Voices in the Briars

Grotesqueries

Hayden Thorne

Published by Hayden Thorne, 2024.

VOICES IN THE BRIARS

*

Copyright © 2024 Hayden Thorne
Cover art © Hayden Thorne

*

Written by Hayden Thorne

*

Also by Hayden Thorne

Arcana Europa
Guardian Angel
The Flowers of St. Aloysius
Hell-Knights
Children of Hyacinth
The Amaranth Maze
A Murder of Crows

Curiosities
Dollhouse
Automata

Dolores
Ambrose
Echoes in the Glass
A Dirge for St. Monica

Ghosts and Tea
The Ghosts of St. Grimald Priory
Agnes of Haywood Hall
A Most Unearthly Rival

The Haunted Inkwell
The House of Creeping Dolls
The Heart of Ameinias
Ada and the Singing Skull
The Dubious Commode

Grotesqueries
A Castle for Rowena
The Rusted Lily
Primavera
The House of Ash
Nightshade's Emporium
Voices in the Briars
The Perfect Rochester
Compline
The Twilight Lover
Doppelgänger

Masks
Masks: The Original Trilogy
Curse of Arachnaman
Mimi Attacks!
Dr. Morbid's Castle of Blood
The Porcelain Carnival

Standalone
Renfred's Masquerade
Rose and Spindle
Gold in the Clouds
Helleville

Icarus in Flight
Arabesque
Banshee
Wollstone
The Glass Minstrel
Henning
The Twilight Gods
The Book of Lost Princes
The Winter Garden and Other Stories
Desmond and Garrick
The Cecilian Blue-Collar Chronicles

Table of Contents

Chapter 1

Lóránt crouched on the riverbank, eyes wide as his gaze followed the moon's reflection on the gently rippling water. Crickets chirped around him, their odd but cheerful song broken now and then by the distant hooting of an owl. The night was clear, the vast sky unbroken by clouds, and the moon hung in a bold circle above. Lóránt loved the silver light, the way it blanketed everything when the moon was full. There was something soothing about it, comforting his aching heart though it might not fix the pain everywhere else.

A stray leaf lay nearby, and he reached for it and carefully leaned forward to set it on the water. In another moment he was watching the soft current carry the leaf away, the moon's reflection a shining and irregular path drawing the leaf toward some unknown destination. And adventure, of course. Lots of adventures out there in the world.

And as his thoughts went down that direction, they also turned to the two children who were adopted this morning. Lóránt wondered how they were faring now. Did they like their new families? Did their families like them? Surely they did if they specifically chose those two out of so many. Those two—Lóránt didn't know their names—had been popular among the other orphans and seemed to like everyone. Well, almost everyone.

He shifted when his legs started to cramp and sat down on the riverbank, his gaze still fixed wistfully on the leaf that was now carrying him away in his imagination.

"Lóránt? What're you doing here?" a soft voice called out from the trees behind him.

Lóránt wasn't even startled. He glanced over his shoulder and shrugged.

"Watching the moon," he signed and then pointed at the river.

"Can I join you?"

Lóránt nodded but didn't move aside. It wasn't as if he didn't want to; he simply couldn't. The nurse took care of his knees' bleeding earlier with the proper spell, but they still throbbed a little, and it still hurt when moving his legs. He'd walked funny the rest of the day, which further slowed him down when it came to his chores.

"The bruised tissue under your skin will continue to heal throughout the day, Lóránt, even if the surface wound itself is gone," the nurse had told him. "I've already spoken with Eszter Pesti about your chores, and she's agreed to wait until you're fully healed."

But St. Jerome's kitchen mistress had done nothing of the sort once Miss Fábián's back was turned. Lóránt might not have been told to help gather the soiled dishes from the tables in the dining hall, but he still wiped the long tables down, which required a good deal of stretching and straining on throbbing knees. At the very least he had three other children doing the same, and everyone's combined efforts made the task much less painful and exhausting. Lóránt performed much more slowly because of his injuries, but he managed to get them done with minimal fuss and suppressed tears.

"How are your knees?" the larger boy sitting beside him asked, his voice still quiet and gentle.

Lóránt considered and softly rubbed the affected areas. The rough fabric of his old trousers wasn't comfortable, but he was used to them.

"They're getting better," he signed. "Still hurts a little, though."

"And you're sure you don't know who hurt you?"

Lóránt nodded, a touch alarmed. He did know who'd pushed him hard from behind, cursing him for being in everyone's way and moving too slowly. He was carrying a couple of soiled platters from breakfast, and Bartó and his gang of four were walking behind, their longer strides easily moving them too close at the worst possible moment.

Lóránt had then reached the narrow door that led to the outer court when the group caught up with him, and when he slowed further to make sure he navigated the low stone steps without trouble, Bartó shoved him. Lóránt stumbled, lost his balance, and fell down (mercifully) three stone steps, scraping his knees badly against the rough surface and losing both platters in a terrific crash.

"Stupid mute," someone from the group snarled as Lóránt stared in horror at the shattered crockery.

"Move faster next time!" another one of them snapped.

It would take him a handful of shocked seconds before the pain in both his knees and heart tore silent sobs from him.

The memory still stung even hours after the incident, and he was back on the riverbank, finding comfort in the moon and the water. And now that Dávid

Bodnár found him and forced him not only to remember but to lie as well, the heartache returned tenfold. He tried to take a deep breath to fight off the tide, but it didn't work, and he burst into tears. At least in Dávid's company he didn't need to feel so ashamed of his muteness and the odd sounds that normally came from him whenever he wept hard like this. Dávid himself once described the voiceless gasps as "wheezes", which only hurt even more since it sounded so abnormal.

"Oh—Lóránt, I'm sorry. I didn't mean to make you cry. Here. Come here."

Lóránt was soon wrapped in a warm and firm embrace, the larger and older boy a familiar presence that usually came when Lóránt needed it the most. Dávid knew him too well, it looked like. As if he could sense Lóránt's distress from a distant part of St. Jerome's and ensured he found his friend to see what the matter was.

Whether immediately or hours later, Dávid would always find him and comfort him in his own way. Like a big brother, literally and age-wise. Dávid was twelve years old to Lóránt's seven, and for some mysterious reason, he'd attached himself to an abandoned boy who was born mute.

There was a good deal of movement from Dávid, and before long all was calm around him, and Lóránt realized Dávid had moved so that Lóránt sat in front of him, bracketed by Dávid's legs and held against Dávid's chest by a pair of iron bands that passed for arms. Dávid stayed quiet for a time, allowing Lóránt to tire himself out while offering warmth and solace.

They watched the river for a few more moments like this, the leaf having long vanished from sight, the crickets' chirping occasionally punctuated by Lóránt's hiccupping gasps. The tears were now spent, and Lóránt's shirt was utterly soaked and soiled with tears and snot. And he felt so, so tired and drained.

"I'd like to follow that river someday," Dávid murmured, his chin resting on the top of Lóránt's head. "I'm sure it cuts through some of the best places out there. Like forests and mountains and wild spaces. I'll only sail on the river at night, though. The moon's pretty, isn't it? It seems to be made for the river." Dávid paused. "All right, it's the other way around. The river's made for the moon. I don't think it looks just as magical when the sun's high and shines on it."

Lóránt listened tiredly, his mind now distracted by Dávid's one-sided conversation. Curiosity turned to calm joy, easily overtaking hurt as he settled into the affectionate rambling from his friend. The moon and the river were a very good pair, he realized, and he could think of nothing better than to do what Dávid planned to do himself.

"Can I join you when you go?" he signed—a little awkwardly since he stayed pressed against Dávid's front, and his friend couldn't really see all of his gestures. Realizing this, he patted Dávid's leg emphatically and forced Dávid to move his head so that he could peer over Lóránt's shoulder when Lóránt signed his question again.

"Of course you can! I was going to ask you to come with me, but you have to grow big and healthy to go out on adventures. We don't know what's out there, and we'll be on our own. We've got to be strong to survive, haven't we?"

"But it'll be beautiful out there!"

"Yes, but there's also danger. It's not all rainbows and flowers, Lóránt."

"Yes, it is," Lóránt insisted, his motions now almost stumbling and hurried as excitement grew. "There'll be lots of birds and trees and mountains like those ones."

Dávid laughed. "All right, all right. If you say so. We'll follow the river and all the rainbows we can find along the way. But I still say you need to grow bigger and healthier to be able to follow the river for miles and miles. Can you do that, then? It's my rule for anyone who joins me."

Lóránt considered, frowning. Dávid was a big boy, to be sure—big-boned, robust, and hearty. Lóránt had heard his friend described as large enough to be mistaken for someone older—like a fifteen-year-old or more. He was smart and kind, perhaps not as popular as the children who were nearly worshipped by the others, but Lóránt saw just how Dávid was respected and listened to. Could Lóránt manage to catch up with his friend, grow into the same height and bulk as Dávid in a couple or so years?

"I'll try hard," he signed at length. "But I don't know when you plan to follow the river. I'll be too slow growing up."

"I'll wait for you, then. I promise."

"But what if I never do? I don't want you to wait forever."

Dávid didn't even hesitate in his response. "I'll wait forever."

And that was that. There was a note of finality in his answer, and Lóránt knew he shouldn't argue since it might irritate his friend. He could ill afford to lose Dávid to stupid things that tended to come out of Lóránt's head even though he never meant to sound foolish. The two settled back into comfortable and familiar silence, and Lóránt found himself lulled further by his friend's embrace and protective hold. With the day's draining moments and that night's final, exhausting purging of grief and pain, Lóránt was truly in a state of complete lethargy. He managed a little smile in between yawns, his dimming gaze still fixed on the moon-kissed water.

As he gradually sank into the restful calm of sleep, he thought he could hear Dávid hum, feel Dávid rock ever so slightly, which worked like magic. Lóránt was pulled in, and he was soon lost in dreams filled with a large, round moon casting silver lights on gentle currents, and he sat on a leaf that carried him to distant lands he knew nothing about.

He was promised rainbows, though—the moon said so, anyway, and the moon never lied. Lóránt floated on the river, and then he floated over uneven ground not in a leaf but in a pair of thick arms. Uneven ground gave way to a flatter surface, but the comforting hold never eased. Everything was going to be all right, the moon whispered, and he believed it. He sank back into sleep, and this time his dreams had Dávid standing on the water and beckoning to him with a smile, his figure wreathed in silver.

Chapter 2

The world was nothing more than a wildly spinning mess of color, noise, and pain. Dávid snarled and cursed, his entire body alternately tensing and relaxing though all that did little to buffer the dreadful impact of tangled bodies on stone. His fists kept swinging, his legs furiously seeking purchase as he fought to pin his adversary down so he could pummel the devil out of him.

Bartó Csonka tried—oh, he tried *so hard*—to show just how well-matched they were in a fistfight. He was fifteen, for heaven's sake, and he equaled Dávid in physique, and yet he barely hung on, taking more than he was able to give. His shouts were in equal parts pain and anger while Dávid's were pure fury. Dávid was going to be in trouble with St. Jerome's director, but he didn't give a damn. Around them, the older orphans shouted and cheered in a cacophony of support for either fighter or dismay over the fallout of this fight.

"Stop! Stop! The director's coming!" a terrified voice yelled.

"Let go, you fucking beast!" Bartó howled as two—well, three—more punches landed.

Dávid merely grunted and took advantage of the time between the terrified warning and the inevitable rough handling of the director's assistants, his vision still red, still filled with the sight of a small, scrawny thing sobbing his heart out on the riverbank.

Knowing that Lóránt had been picked on yet again—unprovoked, of course—and hearing the small boy vent his pain in tight wheezes as though the poor thing were being strangled lit that unfortunate fire in Dávid, who could go from hot to cold and back to hot with the snap of a finger. Oh, he knew exactly who'd hurt Lóránt, and he could think of nothing but to smear Bartó Csonka's smirking mug all over the weathered stone of the orphanage's courtyard.

"That's enough!" a woman's voice barked. "Stop it this instant! Csonka! Bodnár! Here, break this up, Tibor! Vilmos, take Bodnár!"

The rough handling came, and Dávid and Bartó were pulled apart. The world stopped spinning though it took a second or two for Dávid's brain to settle back down, and the rage finally eased, albeit slowly. As far as he was concerned, the reckoning wasn't done. When he straightened and tugged his clothes into a relatively neater state, Dávid felt a bitter wave of satisfaction at the sight of a thoroughly roughed up Bartó—bruised with the promise of a stupendous black eye, his lip bleeding. Dávid was under no illusion that he likely appeared just as bad, but knowing he'd exacted justice on Lóránt's behalf made it all worth it.

"What the hell, Bodnár?" Vilmos Gaál, one of the director's assistants, hissed as he gave Dávid's arm a rough shake. "I expected better from you!" One more disappointed yet angry shake followed, and Mr. Gaál sighed heavily. "I'll take you to the nurse after the director deals with you."

"Yes, sir," Dávid replied. He was sorry for disappointing Mr. Gaál and was determined to bear the tongue-lashing he expected in the director's office, but he still regretted nothing about what he'd done to that miserable piece of shit.

Bartó was led away first by Tibor Bokor, the bigger and more terrifying of the director's assistants. When Mr. Gaál followed, still holding Dávid by the arm, Dávid glanced around, his gaze skimming across the gathered older children and adolescents for—ah, there they were.

Bartó's four friends were separated from each other as planned, Dávid's own little gang ensuring those drooling baboons got their relative share of justice though not through a boy's fist. Everyone knew those thugs thought themselves to be ladies' men, and they'd been chasing a few skirts relentlessly since they turned thirteen or somewhere thereabouts. One of them was unfortunate enough to set his sights on Irén Lovász, a twelve-year-old beauty who took shit from no one and who'd proven herself to be Dávid's superior—not in size and brute strength, but in guile and agility.

It was a mere glance at Irén's unfortunate suitor, but it was enough to confirm a bruised cheek and a distinct air of mortification and wounded pride. No doubt the others in the gang sported other marks of female disgust though perhaps one might have gotten his own version of a black eye in the form of a nasty kick in the groin. One of the girls who counted herself in Dávid's corner wasn't above fighting dirty, and he adored her for it. And so Dávid was led away, the director taking up the rear and barking orders for the children to go back to business—which probably meant go back to talking or flirting or doing what young adolescents did to pass the time.

Bartó went first, and Dávid was forced to wait for several dragging minutes in a small adjoining room with Mr. Gaál posted outside the door. And once the door shut behind the gentleman, Dávid leaped from his chair and bolted to the window to peer out.

The main offices of St. Jerome's were situated somewhere in the middle of the ground floor. Their windows looked out at the rear courtyard, which was the play area for the younger orphans. Smaller figures dotted the dreary space, shrieking in laughter as they played and got in their day's exercise. There were a handful who didn't partake for whatever reason, opting instead to enjoy the shade of the few trees growing along the perimeter just inside the high stone walls.

Lóránt was easy to spot because his movements were predictable. He rarely, if ever, played with his peers and instead sat in the shade and watched. Likely daydreamed, Dávid corrected himself with a pleased little smile that tugged at his now swollen lip and made him wince. Lóránt always daydreamed whenever he wasn't being forced to work by the kitchen mistress—a clear indication of his standing among everyone.

Orphans and abandoned children deemed early on to be impossible to adopt were consigned to kitchen support duties, and when old enough, they'd be offered up for apprenticeship in different trades, the local guilds coming by to pick their new workers for training.

Dávid himself had seen a splendidly dressed representative from some noble household come by in the evening to discuss matters with the director. Then within a week or on the same night, one of the kitchen support orphans who'd grown too old by this point and who was now assigned other housekeeping duties elsewhere in St. Jerome's would be bundled into a waiting carriage, never to be seen again.

Dávid's chest ached at the thought that Lóránt's future was already set. It was no small wonder the boy was barely taught reading and writing while the other children were required to do more and learn basic manualism since they were expected to be able to adapt to a broader range of experiences beyond the orphanage walls. Dávid had long discovered a smaller and more personal value to his own knowledge and growing skill, and he loved seeing Lóránt's face glow from happiness whenever the younger boy was able to communicate dearly held ideas to Dávid without trouble.

"You're very good at signing, too," Lóránt once quipped.

"I have to if I want to keep up with you," Dávid replied, preening, though in truth, only Lóránt depended more on manualism.

Dávid spent the next several minutes simply watching the goings on outside though much of that time was dedicated to keeping an eye on Lóránt's solitary figure in the shade. And wondering why he'd been so drawn to the little thing. Dávid sighed as he considered.

He remembered that time when he was five, and a good deal of hubbub rippled through the head staff during dinner over an infant abandoned on the orphanage's doorstep. Wrapped in rough wool, tucked inside a basket, the baby was notable largely for its silent cries and the single handwritten note slipped inside its swaddling clothes: *Lóránt Kárpáthy, two months. Born mute.* Dávid could still remember the looks exchanged between a couple of the cleaning maids that evening when odd whispers flew about the new baby.

Dávid then didn't really know what was happening, but the look on those girls' faces were seared in his memory because they weren't looks of worry for the unfortunate infant, but of terror. Now that he was much older and able to look back and think upon it with a little more knowledge of the world, he wondered *why* such naked terror on a baby's behalf. Or was it fear *because* the baby was born mute? Was it a sign of bad luck for the orphanage and everyone in it that a mute child was abandoned there? Dávid's temper stirred once again.

"Fucking idiots," he muttered.

The door suddenly opened, and Mr. Gaál peeked in. "It's your turn, Bodnár."

With a sigh, Dávid abandoned the window and was led to the next room. Mr. Gaál again took his position outside the office door though for what purpose, Dávid didn't know since he wouldn't pose a threat to the director. Bullying shits like Bartó and his gang, yes, but not the director.

"For heaven's sake," she said without preamble as she replaced a bejeweled bottle on a nearby shelf. "I do wish you'd take matters up with me first before letting your fists do the talking. What on earth were you thinking, beating the stuffing out of Bartó?"

"He hurt Lóránt without reason because he's a bully, and I don't like seeing other people picked on because they're smaller or weaker," Dávid replied evenly. "I'm sorry for embarrassing you and St. Jerome's, ma'am, but I'm not sorry I beat the shit out of him."

"Tut, language! We aren't teaching you to talk like a ruffian, let alone behave like one, Dávid Bodnár," the director retorted. "And I'll have you know we have families who've applied for Bartó and his friends, and you reducing them to a collection of bruises and broken noses and endangering their status as adoptees is undermining everything St. Jerome's stands for."

"I'm sorry, ma'am. I didn't know..." But Dávid held back the rest. Indeed, had he known, he'd have held his temper in check which would have facilitated a hastier removal of the useless brutes from the orphanage.

"Of course you didn't realize. You act before you think, and I'm afraid your temper will get the better of you someday, Dávid. For heaven's sake, you're only twelve years old, yet you think and act like someone twice your age!"

Dávid winced. Yes, he realized that now, but he couldn't help himself, for that was how things worked in such an environment, wasn't it? It was every man for himself in an orphanage, even in one as well-run and strictly regulated as St. Jerome's. And he did have a temper, but more often than not, it expressed itself when injustice was clearly being played out right in front of him.

It was also a great deal more roused when that injustice was directed at Lóránt. Dávid realized he regretted nothing, would never regret the work of his fists if it meant defending Lóránt though he might not fully comprehend why—why all this trouble for a small, weak, daydreaming mute.

Chapter 3

Outsiders—really hopeful parents—appeared on occasion at St. Jerome's. Sometimes they came in larger numbers that sent the orphanage staff scurrying and the director's terrifying figure emerging from her office and moving among the children. Those outsiders were also entertained and fed in the main dining hall with Lóránt and the other kitchen helpers scrambling to prepare the tables and clean them afterward.

Now and then they'd be called upon to bring another plate of something—bread and cheese, mostly—or carry another pitcher of water to replace the empty one. In the meantime, the director and her assistants chatted with their guests and did their best charming them into observing and, with some luck, meeting children.

Lóránt or his fellow helpers sometimes caught these guests' attention, but the director was always quick to dissuade them.

"They're for the guilds," she'd vaguely say, which Lóránt at first didn't quite understand. But over time he'd heard enough to know he and his companions were reserves meant to (as the director often described it) "bolster the kingdom's economy" with "good apprentices" who were expected to "rise up the ranks" and eventually be journeymen. For his part, Lóránt had absolutely no idea what he'd be good for other than kitchen duties, and Mrs. Pesti often reassured him he'd be moving on to other things once the older reserves were taken in by local artisans and left open positions elsewhere in the orphanage.

"Maybe I can learn to cook, and then I can be like Mrs. Pesti someday and cook for a nobleman," Lóránt signed, smiling shyly at Dávid one evening by the moonlit river. "I've gotten better at cleaning the tables now, and she said I'm very quick at serving guests. And I heard half of the reserves were picked up by people who live in castles to work there."

Dávid watched his gestures with his own thoughtful little smile. "I think you deserve much better than that," he replied, and Lóránt's heart sank.

"But I don't know anything else, and I'm already nine." Lóránt stared at his hands sullenly. He tried to move them to form more words, but his own thoughts dissolved under the weight of disappointment, so he simply laced his fingers together and turned his attention back to the river and the crescent moon above.

"You'll learn more, I'm sure. You're able to read a little more now, and if you keep at it, you'll be able to be more than just kitchen help when the time comes."

Lóránt blinked and glanced up at Dávid, who sat beside him.

"What's wrong with kitchen help? I'm good at it," he demanded, hands flying, gestures a touch agitated. "Mrs. Pesti said every role means something and is important because every person does work that keeps things running well." He tried to sign the exact words used by the kitchen mistress even though they seemed a little odd in his head—a bit too complicated, anyway.

He hoped his best friend wasn't about to turn on him and be another Bartó Csonka. Lóránt had suffered too much already for as long as he could remember. Bartó and his gang might have already been adopted by their families (and thank the stars for that!), but their presence and endless bullying of Lóránt until the glorious days of their adoptions had left scars in Lóránt that would never go away. It would be awful if Dávid were to step in and carry on with the endless battery on Lóránt's heart without doing anything physically hurtful. Words were just as wounding as fists or open palms—perhaps even more so, he found.

"Nothing's wrong with kitchen help," Dávid said at length, and he sighed heavily. "I'm sorry. I shouldn't have said that. I just wanted you to be happy." Then he wrapped an arm around Lóránt's shoulders and gave them a comforting squeeze. An awkward pause followed, and Dávid spoke again in a more subdued voice. "Lóránt—it's my turn to be adopted."

Lóránt stared at him. "Oh. Did you meet them today?"

"A week ago, actually. I didn't think anything of it when they interviewed me, but they returned today and signed papers and all that. I'll be leaving in three days."

Lóránt nodded, blinking, and turned his attention back to the moonlit river. He didn't quite know what to say or how to take this sudden news, but a strange hollowness now filled him.

"Will you write me when you're gone? You said I'm better at reading now, and I promise I'll do that when I get your letters," he signed. His gestures felt unnaturally jerky—as though his hands moved on their own, animated by something outside him.

"I'll visit. I think that'll be better, right? But I'll make sure to write you in between visits." Dávid swallowed audibly. "I'm sorry, Lóránt."

"I'll be all right. It'll be my turn someday." Hopefully sooner than later once he was of age, he now thought as fear slowly, slowly set in. What would he do without Dávid in St. Jerome's? He had no other friends, his fellow kitchen helpers being nothing more than companions with whom he'd exchange a few words now and then but never really enjoyed a moment like this. Nobody knew how to sneak out of the orphanage to sit on the riverbank and marvel at the river at night. Nobody understood Lóránt the way Dávid seemed to understand him, and now Dávid was leaving.

Dávid again moved and settled himself behind Lóránt, and Lóránt's heart broke at the familiar and loving embrace. This would be the last time they'd be watching the river like this, Dávid holding him protectively from behind, his thick legs and arms keeping Lóránt from the dangers of the untamed environment beyond the orphanage walls.

"How come you didn't tell me about your family coming last week?" he asked in heavy, listless gestures.

"I didn't really think anything was going to happen. I've been seen before, remember? I think four families talked to me in the past, and they chose someone else instead. I'm tired of talking about it, I suppose." Dávid shrugged, and Lóránt sighed on his friend's behalf. "Truth be told, I've given up and wondered about probably leaving St. Jerome's like some do when they turn sixteen and apply to find their way in the world pretty much on their own. I was getting myself ready for it in my head and was already putting together a proper plan."

Until the family who'd seen him returned that day—much to Dávid's surprise and Lóránt's dismay. But Lóránt shouldn't grieve, he told himself. If he were in Dávid's shoes, being adopted by people who wanted him would be the best thing to happen, and he wouldn't feel so lonely.

Lóránt knew about his own history—his wretched abandonment at only two months of age. Whether or not it was because he was born mute or if it was because of a host of different factors that worked against his mother's desire to keep him, he didn't know. He'd never know. Dávid, though, enjoyed a significant advantage given his intelligence and his physical strength and especially his kindness. He deserved all the best life could give him considering what he'd done for Lóránt over the years.

"I'll miss you," Lóránt signed at length.

"I'll miss you, too." Dávid pressed a kiss to the side of Lóránt's head. "Promise me you'll take good care of yourself until I see you again. We'll still be following the river in the moonlight, someday. I promise."

Lóránt nodded, unable to communicate anything more, and nothing but silence fell on the two for the rest of their time together. When he settled under the covers in the reserves' dormitory later, Dávid's sudden news finally broke Lóránt's weakened defenses, and he cried himself to sleep.

His friend would be leaving in three days, and until then, Dávid was going to be busy packing his things and getting extra attention from the director and the staff—instructions on how to behave, Lóránt heard, in addition to a few more hours in the schoolroom to ensure Dávid was given the maximum amount of learning in such a short amount of time. He wasn't going to have any time to spare for Lóránt, and Lóránt took care to keep himself busy in turn to avoid thinking about his friend.

On the evening before Dávid's departure, a gentleman in rich clothes under a heavy cloak paid the orphanage a visit. Lóránt was quick to learn that this guest was a nobleman—a Count Boros from the "misty eastern mountains" who'd occasionally come by for young people to add to his staff and who was the director's most valuable guest. Lóránt had never seen Count Boros up close before, but the nobleman had been to visit a few times since Lóránt first came to St. Jerome's, and Lóránt was far too young still to be of any use in the kitchen.

For the count, Lóránt was instructed to bring a couple of pewter goblets to the director's office immediately.

"Be quick, child. He's not one for sluggards," a harried Mrs. Pesti ordered, and Lóránt was all but flying down the passageway with the goblets in hand.

Mr. Gaál opened the door for Lóránt, and he was soon being urged to surrender the goblets on the director's desk. It was cleared of ledgers and ink bottles and on it now stood a dark, gem-encrusted bottle of wine the count had apparently brought. Lóránt tried not to look around as he hurried to the desk, acutely aware of the silence that had fallen on his entrance and the attention he was now receiving from the strangely dressed nobleman. The director appeared not to notice anything odd and proceeded to uncork the bottle once Lóránt placed the goblets down.

"What's your name?" Count Boros suddenly asked, his voice a low and quiet hum floating out of the shadows of his cloak's hood.

Startled, Lóránt froze where he stood and blinked up at their guest. He shook his head and pointed at his mouth before signing his name. Count Boros seemed surprised but recovered himself quickly enough to nod in understanding, his manner now curious and keen, and he leaned a little toward Lóránt.

"Lóránt Kárpáthy? Yes? How old?"

"Nine, sir," Lóránt signed, glancing nervously at the director, who was now watching the proceedings with unusual interest. Her gaze on Lóránt was sharp and questioning—unblinking. Unnerving. He quickly turned his attention back to Count Boros. "I'll be ten in two months."

For a moment no one said a word, and the air felt tense and thick, as though the director and Mr. Gaál were waiting for something momentous to happen and were holding their breaths. For his part, Count Boros continued to stare hard at Lóránt, his face obscured by his overly heavy cloak though Lóránt could glimpse the white lower face in the shadows.

"Eight years, then. That won't be long," Count Boros said after a moment before dismissing Lóránt with a careless wave of a gloved hand and turning back to the director. "Splendid work as always, madam."

Chapter 4

Dinner was long over, and everyone was winding down and readying for bed. Dávid, however, couldn't sit still, and he didn't want to stick around the other orphans and be reminded of friendships that were about to be cut short. He certainly hoped none would be, but no one could tell what the future had in store for him—or for anyone else, at that. And so while the older children washed up and chatted tiredly in their dormitories, Dávid slipped out to take a few turns in the front courtyard.

A few clouds partially obscured the moonlight but did very little to throw the world into complete darkness. There was enough light cast by the few spelled torches scattered around the courtyard to guide Dávid's steps and offer him faint comfort. He strolled along the courtyard's perimeter, his mind quite sunk in melancholy thoughts, unable to help itself whenever it drifted in Lóránt's direction.

Dávid hadn't seen his friend for three whole days, and he wished he could see him then, but Lóránt had been needed in the kitchen for the past week—more so than ever since families seemed to come for the children in what felt like endless waves. The kitchen staff and their hapless little helpers were being run ragged from what Dávid heard, and he desperately hoped poor Lóránt wasn't going to drop from exhaustion when Dávid couldn't be with him to see to his care.

"Psst! Dávid! What're you doing out here?" a girl's voice whispered harshly from the deeper shadows of the trees he'd just passed.

"What the—who's there? Oh, is that you, Irén?" he asked. A familiar face emerged from the gloom, grinning, and Dávid jogged over to join his friend. "I can't rest. I'm trying to wear myself down so I can sleep properly."

"Same here. I'm leaving tomorrow, too, but after lunch." Irén sighed and glanced around. "I'm going to miss this place though I'm heartily glad I'm leaving."

A family of academics who'd recently moved from Warsaw had applied for Irén, their adoption of the girl being a great deal quicker than that of the family who'd seen Dávid. No, he reminded himself, wincing. No, he really ought to start referring to them by name and to get used to being called Dávid Gárdonyi as well. Irén had already begun calling herself Irén Stasiuk and was exceeding-ly comfortable about it. Dávid wished he had half his friend's easy confidence when it came to such monumental changes.

The two chatted amiably for a few minutes, content to lose themselves in their quiet bubble until movement in the courtyard drew their attention away from each other. Dávid, acting on instinct, withdrew further into the shadows while peering out and pulled Irén back with him.

"What's that?" she asked. "Oh—it's that coach again."

A handsome coach that gleamed in the slightly dampened moonlight had just appeared, moving into view with four black horses pulling it. The driver was thickly muffled against the elements though perhaps overly protected so that his face seemed to be nothing more than a white speck in a larger and more shapeless black form. The horses turned as they pulled the coach until they faced the courtyard's entrance and stopped to wait.

And for the next few moments the scene felt as though it were caught in amber because an absolute stillness descended. None of the horses swished their tails or nodded their heads, and neither did the driver shift on his high perch.

"How strange," Irén whispered beside him. "Do you hear that? It's so quiet out here. Too quiet, even, as if all the night animals suddenly hid themselves. I've never experienced anything like this before."

"I know. Wait—here comes someone."

The front double doors swung open, spilling golden light outside, and a lone figure strode out. Like the coach driver, it was heavily and unusually bun-dled against the elements though it was a warm night, and it stopped beside the coach to wait, its attention turning to the open doors. In another moment a smaller and more active figure scurried out, carrying a small bag while dressed in traveling clothes and not the orphanage's coarser uniform.

In the light of the spelled torches, Dávid glimpsed the face and recognized the girl—one of the older reserves who'd been laboring for a few years now, cleaning the dormitories including the communal toilets. She was born with a cleft palate and endured some of the worst bullying from other orphans, and Dávid couldn't blame her for erecting a fiery wall around herself. No one dared talk to her save for St. Jerome's staff, and she was prone to lashing out in red-hot fury at anyone who came close.

And Dávid recognized the silent figure standing by the equally silent coach-and-four. It was that representative from some grand household who'd come by every so often to take one of the reserves away, most likely to be a part of the large army of servants hired to maintain some aristocratic family. He'd never learned the name of the family the figure represented, but he never really cared to. The anxiety and excitement in the girl could be seen, even felt, from where Dávid hid. He couldn't blame her, to be sure, given her history in the orphanage, and with any luck, she was now destined for a far better treatment in her new situation.

She said not a word the whole time, but her face was flushed with high emotion, and when the cloaked man opened the coach door for her, she beamed a grateful smile and clambered awkwardly inside. The man followed with ease and swiftness, and then the coach-and-four were moving off.

Dávid waited as did Irén, and once he was sure they were once again alone, he let out a breath he didn't even know he'd been holding. A glance at his friend revealed the same tension being released, and they shared nervous smiles. The night around them came alive as well, crickets softly filling the air along with the evening breeze.

"Lucky her," he said at length, but for some reason, he didn't feel anywhere close to how he thought he ought to feel in this instance.

There was no real relief there, and in spite of the girl's clear happiness at being chosen, Dávid couldn't shake of a vague sense of dread on her behalf. He couldn't understand it himself. And no matter how much he turned his odd response to the proceedings, he remained just as baffled as ever. What Irén said after another moment of silence certainly didn't help matters, either.

"Did you notice anything strange about the coach?" she asked, her voice quiet and doubtful.

"They stood like statues, you mean?"

"Not that—I mean, they did, yes, which is pretty strange on its own, but—when they moved, they didn't make a single sound. Tell me you noticed it because I don't want to think I'm going insane."

Dávid had to pause and consider, now startled by his friend's observation. "I—damn, you're right. I knew there was something off about the whole thing! We're not both delusional at the same time, are we? That's impossible, anyway, and—fuck me. What does it mean?"

"I don't know. But—but maybe there's a logical explanation for it."

Irén didn't sound convinced, but she'd always been the more grounded one of the two, and Dávid knew better than to question her claims. She was also quite the scholar and the skeptic, constantly challenging and questioning the world around them, and it was no wonder intellectuals had moved swiftly to apply for her.

They soon returned to their respective dormitories, embracing tearfully one last time and exacting promises to write. Irén would easily discover Dávid's new address, of course, because she was very much a sleuth-hound in addition to being a scholar, and she was more likely to write him first. Dávid was fine with it, really.

Once snug under his covers, he could barely keep his mind from chasing after so many things, and now excitement and anxiety were making way for a wholly different emotion: foreboding. That vague apprehension he'd felt after watching the wretched girl get carried off in a rich coach not only refused to leave him be, it seemed to have worsened considerably in a matter of an hour or so. And try as he might, Dávid simply couldn't shake it off though he was still at a loss as to why he'd feel such trepidation on the girl's behalf.

So he tried to draw his thoughts away by fixing them on Lóránt instead, seeking relief and comfort in his little friend's growing confidence and strength—if not physically, then mentally. The years had passed so quickly, and what a difference those years made in the boy. Dávid could picture Lóránt growing up and turning into a handsome youth—perhaps still pale and slight but hiding a wealth of lovely surprises, and Dávid was confident his friend would best him in ways that mattered when physicality and brute strength fell short. As he drifted off, finally, he regretted not being able to say goodbye to the dear little thing, his heart aching so badly.

His new fathers didn't waste a minute once the sun rose the following morning. Messrs. Gárdonyi arrived in their own coach, greeting the director and Mr. Gaál in a manner that was distinctly gentlemanly but touched with a world-weariness that wasn't lost on Dávid.

The married pair had traveled extensively all over the continent as far as Dávid knew, and they were also quite built like he was—tall, broad, and muscular, clearly brought on by years of physical work of some nature. But they were also almost like Irén in their intellectual sharpness, the way with which both gentlemen keenly surveyed the orphanage while chatting with Dávid revealing actively engaged minds that perhaps refused to rest. And Dávid couldn't wait to learn more about his new family.

"We hope you'll like your new home," the gentleman with the white-blond hair and a scar bisecting his left cheek said with youthful energy. He even slapped his thighs once Dávid settled down on the seat across from his new fathers. "It's big enough for five of us—I mean us two, you, and your older sister and brother..."

He and his husband took turns extolling the virtues of Dávid's new home, but their words were lost on him not because of his now heightened state of nervousness and joy, but because he happened to glance out the open window just as the coach began to move.

Standing against the nearest wall of the orphanage, somehow managing to sneak out while everyone was in the dining hall for breakfast, was Lóránt. He watched the coach, his large, expressive eyes fixed resolutely on the window, his figure so fragile against the harsh gray stone. He couldn't spot Dávid even from that distance, but the painful hope in that gaze made Dávid think of their moon-kissed river and the promise of following it together someday.

"I'll see you again, Lóránt," he murmured, swallowing back the threatening tears. "I swear I'll never forget you."

Lóránt raised a pale hand in farewell just before he vanished from view when the coach turned and rumbled out of St. Jerome's courtyard.

Chapter 5

The days felt long and empty following Dávid's departure from St. Jerome's, and Lóránt didn't even know how he managed to survive them with just the usual tasks. Somehow he did, but perhaps it was the numbness and complete disinterest he had in everything around him that must have helped. Lóránt simply stopped caring, shutting himself out of the world even more and for once feeling grateful for being born mute. His physical limitation worked like a proper shield against attention from everyone, and he really didn't have to try so hard to ignore them all.

Let them ignore him in turn, continue thinking of him as an idiot because of his inability to speak. The occasional insult and taunt came for him, of course, but now that he'd turned ten and found himself very much alone, his indifference strengthened his desire to lose himself in tedium. He even stopped sitting on the riverbank because it brought back far too many memories of his friend.

The first letter from Dávid arrived when the air turned chilly, and snow began its reign.

Lóránt stared at his friend's scrawl—rather crooked and rough, actually, and even Dávid himself had joked about his terrible penmanship—his eyes filling with tears. He wished he could read the letter's contents, and while he appreciated Dávid's efforts at fulfilling a promise, he couldn't help but weep over his nearly negligible reading ability. Some basic words were perfectly fine, but the rest flew well above his head though he could mentally pronounce the words as long as he recognized each letter.

Scrubbing his eyes dry with his jacket's sleeve, Lóránt wondered if he could persuade someone to read Dávid's letter to him. Would his friend mind having his private thoughts revealed to someone else, when they were meant solely for Lóránt? Surely he wouldn't be offended, knowing Lóránt's miserable lack of a proper education. So with that in mind, Lóránt knew exactly where to take the letter though he made sure to wait for the right time to invade her privacy.

Miss Fábián was enjoying a break from caring for the children in her sick room when Lóránt came by.

"Begging your pardon, Miss Fábián, but I was wondering if you could read Dávid's letter for me," Lóránt signed. "It just arrived, and I can't read all of it because I don't know how."

The nurse appeared surprised at first but then quickly set her cup of hot tea aside and smile gently at him, a hand outstretched. "No need to be worried," she replied. She was always so kind toward Lóránt, even sneaking him a small sweetbread, decadent roll, or biscuit on occasion to help him "bulk up" because he made her think of a reed. "I always have time for you, my dear. Now come—let's see what our dashing young Dávid has to say."

Lóránt happily perched himself on a stool and waited as Miss Fábián skimmed the letter at first before going back and reading out loud.

"Dear Lóránt, I'm now situated at my new home with my new family. I have two fathers, an older brother named Ambrus, and an older sister named Éva. Ambrus is twenty-one, and Éva is nineteen. It's rather funny, but we are all big and strapping except for Éva, but she's very tall all the same and is very intimidating in her own way. We have one dog and one cat, and I find myself playing with both much more than spending time exploring my new home. It's an old and very big house that stands on the side of a road and is built on a mountainside or something. It's hard to describe, but I hope you'll get to see it someday when you're finally independent.

"I'm actually thinking of requesting that you be given a few days' leave so you can visit, and my fathers said that should be possible. My new family is well-read and know a lot about the history and lore of the Kingdom of Hungary and everywhere else, and the library is packed with so many books that I'm expected to read. I was told it's necessary for me to continue my education this way, and in addition to the usual general stuff we were taught in St. Jerome's, I'm now to learn history and other things. I'll write you again, hopefully soon. I do miss you and hope to see you again. For now, take care and remember your promise to eat a lot and grow up healthy and strong because we still have that river trip to do in the future. With much love, Dávid."

Lóránt had started crying all over again at the sound of Dávid's words, his mind working hard to add his friend's voice to Miss Fábián's reading. He missed his dearest friend so badly, it simply hurt to receive a letter and still not be able to read it the way most people around him could read. But reserves for the guilds weren't given the same amount of attention by way of education, and only the most basic reading and writing lessons were doled out to them.

The reserves' tutor merely shrugged when asked, saying it wasn't necessary for them to be fully literate where they were headed. Blacksmiths, carpenters, bakers, and whatnot didn't care for anything but a skilled pair of hands helping them. In fact, literacy meant risk because people who could read and comprehend more were likely to want more than what had been allotted to them, and therein would always lie trouble.

"I don't know how to write back," Lóránt signed after he calmed down. Miss Fábián also took care to soothe him with gentle words and his own cup of tea. "I can write a little. Nothing as long and fancy-sounding as what Dávid wrote."

"You know you can always come to me for help. Oh, I'm not going to write your letters for you, child, but I can steer you while you do it." Miss Fábián smiled—a fond, parental smile, in fact—and brushed Lóránt's hair with tender fingers. "Just let me know ahead of time when you think you'll be needing me, and I'll set aside some time for you. All right?"

Lóránt nodded, sniffling and grinning back in sheer relief. "Thank you."

With the nurse's unexpected show of support and encouragement, Lóránt's depression lifted though his shields remained. Perhaps not as strongly as before now that hope had lit a fire in his breast, and he had something to look forward to. No, it might not replace Dávid completely, but a correspondence between them would at least bolster Lóránt's low spirits and help him see through each day, through each dreary task as his day's chores lengthened with his advancing years.

Less than a week after receiving Dávid's letter, when the snow fell and the icy wind howled outside the orphanage's walls, Lóránt was summoned to the director's office. After an unusual round of stiff pleasantries, she plunged ahead with the reason behind this surprising visit.

"I've been tasked to see to your education and improvement, Lóránt," she said as she sat behind her desk, hands clasped on its gleaming surface.

She pinned Lóránt in his chair with an icy blue gaze, her pale features appearing spectral in her dimly lit office. And for once, Lóránt wished one of her assistants were present since she always terrified him with her distant and unyielding presence, and he cowered in spite of himself.

"You're to spend more time in the company of a tutor specifically chosen for you—not the one for reserves, but a new one your patron hired for this purpose."

Patron? Lóránt blinked. He didn't know what a patron was and was too afraid to ask, so he merely wrung his hands nervously on his lap as he listened.

"And this also means you're no longer one of them—the reserves, I mean. No more kitchen duties, no more household tasks for you, but you're not exactly one of the others, either, since you're not to be adopted."

The director paused, pursing her lips as she considered what to say next.

"Truth be told, young man, I'm not really sure how to categorize you or tell you what your standing is in St. Jerome's moving forward. This has never happened before, but I understand this is a unique situation that likely won't be repeated in the future.

"Suffice it to say, since you're quite behind on literacy, you're expected to spend a great deal more time with your new tutor. Your lessons will be extensive and intense to make up for lost time. There are set expectations by way of results in the future, and it won't do to dally and drag your feet over subjects you don't like or tasks you feel are too difficult. Do you understand? You have a patron who's spending a great deal of money on you, and you ought to remember your place and your obligations for this turn of fortune."

Lóránt swallowed and nodded numbly, his mind scrambling to keep up with this startling development.

"Closer to your fifteenth birthday, we'll be adding lessons on comportment and giving a hand in spiritual guidance. We hope that by that time, you'd have mastered everything you need to know in reading, writing, and mathematics with a wider exposure to history and science—at least the fundamentals in those disciplines, anyway." She paused again. "Have you any questions so far? I know this is quite a bit to take in."

Lóránt shook his head. "None, ma'am. Thank you. I promise to work hard," he signed, his movements awkward and stiff, still unable to fully comprehend what all this meant. All the same, he knew the director was a woman who disliked idle chatter and so kept to quick, direct responses.

She inclined her head in acknowledgment, her own bearing very queenly and cold. Fixed and eternal, even, in a way that felt unnervingly elusive. The warm light from the candles and the nearby fireplace did absolutely nothing to make her more earthbound—warmer and more human. If anything, the golden glow only highlighted her ghostly appearance nearly to an extreme, and Lóránt could barely keep himself from running out of her office in speechless terror. But he could also hear Dávid's cheerful voice chiding him for being such an overly nervous little thing, and he tamped down the urge to flee.

"As a final item, your quarters are to be moved to the north tower. It's your patron's express wish to ensure you keep your mind fixed on your education and your overall improvement. No rough play with your peers is allowed since it means the risk of injuries or illness. There's no room for unnecessary distractions. You're expected to live in relative seclusion for a host of reasons you'll be discovering in the future—too complicated for you to sort out at the moment, I'm afraid. But suffice it to say, you've got your tutor for company and a few other servants who'll be looking to your needs."

The director sighed and moved back to settle herself against her chair's backrest, her gaze fixed on Lóránt still. "It's a very, very strange arrangement, I know, but you'll get used to it. I promise. I'll be coming by regularly to see to your progress and will be available for questions if you have any that only I can answer. It's your patron's will. Now—your new tutor will be arriving tomorrow, so start packing. You've already been released from your duties and will have more time to sort personal things out. Dismissed."

Chapter 6

Dávid peered out of his bedroom window to marvel at the scene beyond. Winter had come, and the mountains looked spectacular in their shroud of white. Ancient trees and even more ancient rocks seemed to fill every bit of available space, adding to the calm isolation of the family home. There was majesty everywhere, Dávid saw, both within and without, and even after a month spent in his new sanctuary, he still couldn't quite get used to it.

Every now and then, he'd catch himself wistfully thinking of Lóránt and imagining his little friend lost in wonder at the sight of ageless and untamed beauty around them. He really would need to speak with his fathers again about visiting Lóránt once the season eased into the gentler temper of spring.

A tap on his hand drew his attention back from the world of daydreams, and he smiled when he glanced down at Piri, the family cat. A muscular white creature with odd-colored eyes in blue and yellow, she'd taken to Dávid nearly the moment he stepped across the threshold, nervous and even a touch terrified. Calm and dignified at all times, she'd become Dávid's shadow wherever he went and even retired with him at the end of the day, her familiar weight on the bed a comforting influence that helped him sleep.

"Time for breakfast, I know," he said as he gently petted her silky head. "Let's go."

His walk downstairs to the dining-room took him past dimly lit corridors lined with large portraits of long-dead family, the lineage going back at least five centuries from what he was told. And the more distant in time, the more vague the likeness—understandably—with emphasis placed more on suggestion and impression rather than accuracy. Given the ridiculous number of faces staring somberly out of their painted canvases, not only was every member of the Gárdonyi family represented, but also the Samsas' to celebrate the two families' joining.

Apa—Zsigmond Gárdonyi, Dávid's blond-haired, scarred parent—came from a family of minor aristocrats, and the house was his. Many of the people represented in the portraits scattered all over the mansion belonged to Pa—Miklós Samsa, the bespectacled and brooding half of Apa's heart.

Dávid's first fortnight with his family was spent listening to story after wild story of how Apa wooed Pa, the inevitable stumbles and mortifying matchmaking efforts of their parents and families once Apa's intentions were known and Pa at first wanted nothing to do with him.

Their adoption of Ambrus at ten years of age and Éva at eight took place a year after their wedding, the children coming from two different orphanages elsewhere in the Kingdom of Hungary. Piri and Matild, the overly energetic Vizsla, were added to the family's numbers as a kitten and a puppy two years before Dávid's adoption.

"And this is it for us," Apa said with a hearty bark of laughter. "No more! Ambrus and Éva have grown up into holy terrors, let me tell you, and we're not getting any younger."

To which Ambrus rolled his eyes and Éva raised an imperious brow. Both of them had been welcoming and warm, each mirroring one of their parents almost to an uncanny degree—as though they were biologically linked. Ambrus was just as gregarious and talkative as Apa while Éva was quieter but just as quick with a good joke or easy banter as Pa. All worked to ease Dávid's transition to family life, and after a month of this, his disbelief over his good fortune finally gave way to happy and grateful acceptance.

Now and then, of course, he couldn't help but think about the small boy he'd left behind, and he would pray fervently for Lóránt's safety and health.

Ambrus and Éva had given Dávid an extensive tour of the house—which turned out to be more of a mansion or a baby castle in Dávid's eyes. And it was an impressive and formidable structure, timeless in its existence (no one knew exactly when it was built) and impressive in its darkly gothic design. When Dávid first wrote to Lóránt, he'd vaguely described the house as something built on a mountainside, and he was correct yet still off the mark in many ways.

Ironically, the longer he lived in it, the less confident he became in his ability to convey everything to his friend in writing other than references to narrow, pointed windows, steeply gabled roofs, two round towers topped with conical spires, gothic arches and niches, and a driveway spanning a rough mountain road below. Apa had gone into extensive detail about the house's architecture and, indeed, history.

"The foundation has extensive prayer-spells carved into it, you know." He also claimed the mansion had been modified and added to over the years to reflect changes in fashion while keeping to the structure's purpose.

As to what that purpose was?

"Protection, of course, of the family and their legacy," Apa replied with a breezy pride that wasn't lost on Dávid. He didn't expand on it further, but something told Dávid there was a great deal more to it than what had been so ambiguously shared.

Dávid cleared his head as he entered the dining-room where his family had already gathered. He went straight for the immense sideboard where hot food awaited his pleasure, and he was soon headed to his assigned chair with a packed plate. Pa watched him with a satisfied air and nodded his greeting.

"Be sure to have some seconds," he said after swallowing and drinking his coffee. "There's plenty to be had."

"I don't think I can eat any more than this," Dávid replied, eyeing his piled food. His fathers had been most insistent at his bulking up, arguing about his biology and how such a naturally big-boned and large boy would require much more food than what he'd grown used to at the orphanage. "I'll throw up, I'm sure, if I force myself."

"Don't listen to them," Éva piped up from the chair beside him. "Apa and Pa just love seeing us stuff ourselves."

"Strength and energy, young lady. Strength and energy. You don't know when they'll come in handy."

"Really, Pa. There are limits, you know. Go on, Dávid, eat what you can, and don't force things."

Dávid ducked his head, abashed, and proceeded to eat his breakfast in silence while easy conversation flowed around him. Apa had a letter beside his plate, and it had his full attention. Dávid at first wondered why no one made a fuss over this obvious dereliction of proper table manners, and he eventually learned it was a common sight at the dining-table. In fact, correspondences Apa would bring to a meal seemed to be held with some odd kind of guardedness. It was as though the letters contained messages that heralded bad events, and everyone else simply carried on with their meal while keeping one ear open to whatever Apa might say about the letters' contents.

So far, Dávid saw nothing else come of those moments with Apa simply refolding the letters and tucking them under his plate before finishing his meal.

That morning, however, was different. There was a distinct gravity in Apa's manner when he read the correspondence, his brows wrinkling a little while he absentmindedly sipped his coffee, and his food sat neglected before him. He also reread the contents more than twice while Pa, Ambrus, and Éva seemed to purposefully ignore him, their morning banter growing stiffer and more self-conscious as the minutes passed. At length, Apa set the letter aside and dove into his breakfast.

"Everything all right, darling?" Pa asked.

Apa glanced up, his gaze briefly on Dávid before settling on Pa. "An answer to my inquiry," he said, which wasn't a proper answer, Dávid thought. "I'll have to go over details with you in the study. Oh, Ambrus? Éva? I need both of you there, too."

Collective understanding seemed to dawn on everyone, and Éva turned to Dávid. "Since your tutor's not expected to arrive in another fortnight, I'll give you a head start on some reading. Have you explored the library yet? Splendid. What about the reliquary room? No? We can start there, then."

Here Éva paused and glanced back at Apa, who was now watching the conversation intently from the head of the table. He gave her a quick nod—an unspoken permission to an unasked request. The gravity in his manner was still there, and she turned to Dávid with a smile.

"It's best to get you started on the family history, Dávid. There's an alcove in the reliquary room that's filled with books and private journals from Apa's family, dating all the way back several generations. I'll have the servants start a fire there and bring up a tray of tea and biscuits if you wish."

Dávid nodded. "I've only been to the reliquary room a couple of times but never really explored it." He paused, hesitating, his face reddening. "I—uh—it's a little frightening. The room is, I mean, because of all the strange things that're in there."

"Of course. Don't worry. Once the spelled sconces are lit and the fire's burning, that room looks quite cheerful. Oh, and you can have Piri and Matild to keep you company as well."

"Aren't you staying with me?"

"Éva will be needed for a little while, darling," Pa cut in with a reassuring little smile. He pressed a hand on Dávid's arm for a gentle squeeze. "But she'll be available afterwards and can join you in the reliquary room if you prefer human company."

Dávid merely nodded his thanks. While he knew having the family pets around truly added some much-needed cheer to such a room, he suspected the usual bravery offered by the power of light from the spelled sconces and the fireplace still required extra help in human form. He'd been to the reliquary room in the past as he'd said, but those times when he did go had left a sour taste in his mouth, and he'd avoided it since.

There was simply something about the reliquary room and its contents that touched something deeper in him in such a way as to terrify him—an unfathomable, primordial horror.

The chamber itself was quite massive and tall, its portrait-lined walls bearing down on him with centuries' old weight of vanished lives, and floor space was partly taken up by several wooden chests and trunks with all sorts of embellishments, every one of them secured with a massive padlock. There were the more monastic types or the sort of reliquaries he'd seen during holy pilgrimages as a child—highly decorated wooden boxes with pitched roofs mirroring church architecture.

However, in this instance, no saintly visage gazed out from painted details or carvings. Any and all identifiable figures and forms were those of dragons, wolves, and demons that made the hair up and down Dávid's body stand on end.

Chapter 7

Mr. Eszes peered through his spectacles and frowned, his attention fixed on the paper he held while Lóránt did his level best not to squirm in his chair. After what felt like an eternity of this, the tutor nodded and looked at him, a faint smile on his face.

"Excellent work," he said, his voice gruff and hard in spite of his pleasure. "You're improving at a faster rate than expected, Lóránt. That means double work for me, I'm afraid, since I'll need to go back and adjust my lesson plans for you yet again."

And Lóránt would have apologized for the trouble had the older gentleman not punctuated his words with an approving nod and a close-lipped smile. "Thank you, sir. I try my best," he signed instead, his face warming.

"You are. It's evident, and it's greatly appreciated." Mr. Eszes glanced at his pocket-watch and nodded. "Ah. Time's also flown, and we're done with your lessons. Now—have you anything you wish me to tell the director? I'm set to meet her for my weekly reports on your progress."

Lóránt shook his head. "I'd like to write a letter to my friend and then take my lunch."

Once he was alone in the private classroom, Lóránt sighed and gathered his books. He was tired from another morning of very intensive work, and his brain throbbed in his skull, but nothing diminished his joy from all the praises his tutor showered him with all week. It was high time for him to share the news with Dávid though he'd yet to receive a response from his last two letters.

It was a touch disappointing, of course, but Mr. Eszes had also chided him for his impatience since Lóránt wrote far more frequently, apparently unable to hold off and allow Dávid enough time to read and respond. For all he knew, Dávid was off yet again with his family, who were quite the adventurers and who were now bringing their youngest child into their plans of exploration and study. Dávid himself wrote back quite a bit over time but nowhere near the frequency of Lóránt's efforts at communicating. At least his correspondences were long and thorough and an absolute joy to read.

And Dávid had yet to visit. It was another disappointment, but with his hours now full, Lóránt found he didn't have time left to mourn. At least Dávid was consistent in his letter-writing, and his energy never flagged. In fact, Lóránt's astonishing improvement in his ability to read and write had impressed and delighted Dávid enough for him to encourage a more regular exchange of letters.

"I'm very sorry I haven't visited yet, but it sounds like you're doing excessively well," Dávid wrote. "Keep up your good work, and your patron will be very proud of you, and before you know it, he'll come by and take you home at last. Has he written you at least since he's yet to pay you a visit of his own?"

That had been one of the initial letters Lóránt received from his friend when his situation changed quite drastically, and he was finally settled in at St. Jerome's north tower. And, no, Lóránt's patron had yet to pay him a visit or even write a letter, but the director was his mouthpiece, and she'd been to see him regularly—once a fortnight, that is, while Mr. Eszes gave her his reports on Lóránt's progress weekly. He'd been discouraged from writing to his patron with accounts of his work as well as expressions of gratitude for the unexpected and keen interest in his well-being and improvement.

"It's enough he hears it from me, young man," the director said in one of her visits, and the subject was raised. "He's well aware in his own way, anyway, or he wouldn't have chosen you."

"Oh. I don't remember meeting him, though," Lóránt signed after a moment's puzzled silence.

"That's neither here nor there at this point," was the abrupt reply. "Just carry on with the good work."

And that was that. Lóránt was once again left alone, conversation and companionship limited to his tutor, who stuck around through lunch but was then replaced by a gloomy old nun who'd been recruited from a nearby convent to look to his spiritual needs and to begin initial work on his comportment. She was at least a good conversationalist in spite of her overly serious manner, surprising Lóránt with her knowledge of the wider world while generously peppering their time together with books on the fantastical and magical.

"Most of these are morality tales," she said with a grim smile.

In her company Lóránt enjoyed stories of what happened in the world—in real life, that is—as well the exact opposite with fireside tales and lore from different corners of Europe. And between the three adults who were now solid presences in his life, Lóránt found he didn't miss the orphanage—not that there was much to miss, anyway, besides Dávid's company.

He'd never formed strong bonds with anyone else, not even with his fellow reserves, though he did occasionally wonder how they were now faring. Inquiries hastily written down for the benefit of servants who would come by with his meals or to clean the north tower yielded information that didn't really vary. All the same, Lóránt was grateful for those brief interactions since the servants were younger and more attuned to the comings and goings of the orphans under the director's care.

"Oh, we just lost so-and-so to a family" or "So-and-so was taken to the castle" or "So-and-so passed away from a lung infection." Lóránt didn't know any of the children mentioned save for the reserves even if only by name, and he was happy on their behalf that they'd be taken to some nobleman's castle for a better life. He would have been one of their numbers, and at times he wondered what his fate might have been had his patron not interceded in this remarkable way.

As for the guilds, no one had yet to say something about them though the director continued her claim of reserves being meant for apprenticeships. And while no one was foolish enough to challenge her dictates in spite of the absence of artisans and craftsmen who'd have benefitted from those orphans' help, Lóránt still heard whispered rumors about St. Jerome's reserves being too "damaged" to be of any use save for the aristocracy, who seemed to snap them up readily enough more frequently than what Lóránt initially believed.

Of course, Lóránt's free time was spent doing anything he wished, which included not just writing long letters to Dávid, but reading different adventure books, practicing art, and exploring the small grounds around the tower.

From one of the bedroom windows—the one that looked out to the mist-shrouded, low mountains beyond the wood—he'd try to catch a glimpse of the castle the reserves were claimed to be brought to. While the distance was great, the castle was still relatively visible on a clear day, a venerable pile of ancient gray stone and round black towers that invited a host of fantastical stories in Lóránt's mind.

Would his and Dávid's moon-kissed river take them to the castle? Lóránt smiled wistfully as he settled himself on the window seat and rested his chin on his arms while he gazed out. It was a lovely, peaceful scene, the distant landscape offering so much promise by way of romance and adventure though the wood growing much closer to his refuge effectively put an end to such fanciful turns. Lóránt tried to avoid glancing down at the old, old oaks lurking just outside the orphanage walls. Their moment would come soon enough, in fact, and when it did, Lóránt would have ensured his protection from the night world by the firm latching of his windows.

"The tower room is awfully lonely at night," he'd written more than once to Dávid. "It's also very frightening when something wakes me up in the middle of the night, and I don't know what it is, and I'm lying in bed, listening in the dark. My tower room doesn't have curtains, but the windows can be locked tightly. The moonlight comes in sometimes, and that helps, but mostly it's so dark and cold. I hear sounds outside that make me think of something moving against the wall of the tower every now and then. I don't know if it's a bat or a bird or something that can fly and can hold on to stone and move over it.

"Sometimes I think I hear something breathing outside my window, too, but I think it's just a dream because I go back to sleep feeling nervous and frightened. I think that makes me dream of strange things, but when morning comes, everything outside looks very normal and pretty. Even the wood looks peaceful even though it still makes me a little nervous just looking at it. It's like the trees are keeping secrets from me, and I don't like that."

Lóránt would take care to throw the casements wide open to air out his bedroom once the sun rose, reveling in the fresh morning breeze regardless of the temperatures. It also allowed him a moment to look down and inspect the outer walls of the north tower, memories of the previous night's odd sounds coming back to remind him.

And, no, there were no hand holds anywhere on the round tower's walls. Not even ivy or other vines could be seen, the groundskeeper doing a thorough job of keeping the structure free of such things. Surely the nocturnal sounds that unsettled Lóránt late at night were nothing more than hallucinations of some sort impressing themselves in a mind straddling wakefulness and sleep.

"You were always the one with the colorful imagination of the two of us," Dávid would respond in his letters, fondness dripping from every word and making Lóránt's throat tighten in that familiar way. "As long as you keep your windows locked securely, you shouldn't have any problems with night birds or bats. Not that I blame any of those creatures, anyway, Lóránt. I'm sure so many things outside your tower would be drawn to you should you step outside the walls, and not all of them will be friendly. So behave and keep to your tower for safety since I'm not there to protect you anymore like I used to."

Lóránt blinked at the suggestion of unfriendly intentions toward him since wild creatures were almost always wary of humans and either protected themselves by being threatening or by simply vanishing from sight.

Now look who's being silly, he thought, rolling his eyes and smiling as he reread his friend's letter before pressing a fond kiss to the missive and carefully folding it and securing it in a small box with its own lock. It was rapidly filling with letters from Dávid, and Lóránt knew he'd have to plead for a larger box or maybe even a second box of a similar size from the director soon.

Life settled into a steady beat of quiet predictability that suffused Lóránt's heart with a calm happiness he hadn't known while in the main orphanage, and boredom had become a curiously distant idea. He'd never realized till his move to the north tower just how starved he was for knowledge, and he found he never tired of books and conversation, never loathed long, droning lectures and the occasional sharp corrections. Though he easily fatigued from the task, he also learned just how much he loved writing his thoughts down, his letters to Dávid being more than just happily shared accounts of his experiences. They'd become his private journals that revealed much more than what was mundane, and only Dávid seemed to hold the key that opened his heart and soul in ways Lóránt had never thought of before.

Chapter 8

The sound of the carriage rumbling across the stone driveway finally broke through the hollow silence of the library, and Dávid's spirits rose. It had been a week since his entire family packed and left in a hurry, solemn whispers exchanged between them, and Dávid being left out in the cold as to their reason for this sudden burst of activity.

Such a scene happened several times already since Dávid was brought home from St. Jerome's, but he was given strict orders to stay behind and carry on with his education, his venerable tutor not at all given to sympathy or pity toward a lonely adolescent.

"You'd do well to honor your fathers' command, young man," Mr. Szarka would usually say when Dávid was in a bit of a petulant mood. "Both your siblings had to be stuck at home when they were your age, doing exactly what you're doing right now."

"Will I be allowed to join them when I'm older, then?" Dávid asked—no, grumbled—as he sagged in his chair while Mr. Szarka glared at him, unimpressed. "They don't even talk about what they do other than important business related to the family vocation or something like that. I know Ambrus and Éva are being groomed to take over someday, and they're just as tight-lipped as Apa and Pa. I'm going to be groomed someday, too, aren't I?"

Mr. Szarka merely sighed and pinched his mouth, nudging his spectacles up his nose. "You know far more than I, I'm afraid, but if that's the course your brother and sister are taking, it's safe to assume your turn will come soon enough. Well, once you're done with all this, and your fathers are satisfied with the results."

Dávid nodded, sighing. Well, that wouldn't be for another few years, he thought, deflated. He was never as quick and sharp as Irén or many of his peers back at St. Jerome's, and that included his dear Lóránt, the remembrance of whom never failed to draw a wistful smile from Dávid. Yes, even Lóránt, for all the neglect in his early education, clearly had what it took to best Dávid in all things intellectual with hardly any sweat breaking. Dávid had glimpsed his friend's mental acuity several times over the few years spent together, and it was only the director's unfair rules that had stymied poor Lóránt's intelligence and discouraged his efforts. Her orders as well as all prejudices toward a child who was born mute, specifically, turned into fatal bed partners in Lóránt's case.

Dávid received several letters from his friend since the sudden and unexpected turn in Lóránt's fortune, for which Dávid celebrated. And the resulting letters—their contents as well as the rapidly improving quality of Lóránt's writing—were testament to Lóránt's suppressed gifts. Dávid missed his friend so much, but he simply couldn't pay him a visit with his fathers proving to be extremely strict guardians despite their clear love for him. They lived too far, anyway, and it grieved Dávid to no end that he'd be breaking such an important promise to Lóránt.

The sound of the front door opening and the entry hall filling with his family's tired but happy voices put a stop to Dávid's mental wandering, and he hurried out of the library to meet them.

"Tsk! No running, Dávid!" Apa good-naturedly barked when Dávid all but leaped through the doorway to land in his father's welcoming arms. "You're seventeen now and should be behaving more like a proper gentleman. Ah—we missed you, darling. It's good to be home."

Dávid held on tightly, unabashed at being so emotionally impulsive, a trait that had seen some improvement over time. At least he no longer picked fights the moment he sensed an injustice done, and his family had taken great care to ensure that he curbed such a fierce tendency—redirect his temper down a far better, far more productive outlet. It was simply too bad they also insisted upon his ongoing studies to be such an outlet when Dávid had been growing more and more aware of being a man of action and less a man of quiet, intellectual pursuits. Indeed, his tutor would wholeheartedly and grudgingly attest to that.

"How was the trip?" he asked, trying not to sound so pathetic and needy when he embraced Pa next. "And when can I come with you? I'm tired of being left alone all the time."

"All the time? Hardly! These business trips only happen, what, once a month at most?" Pa replied, laughing and embracing him back. He pulled away and kissed Dávid's forehead, holding him at arm's length and observing him closely. "Did you have a growth spurt again while we were away? You'll be taller than all of us by the time you stop growing! Good lord! Zsigmond! Did you notice the boy's height? I could swear he was four inches shorter before we left."

"We're a family of giants," Ambrus said, echoing Pa's laughter. He moved past them, briefly pausing to greet Dávid with a kiss on the cheek, a stuffed satchel hanging down his side. Dávid noticed how exhausted and drawn his brother was, but the light in his eyes was bright, indicating a business successfully concluded.

Éva, greeting Dávid similarly, also carried an overly stuffed satchel—a familiar sight now though at first Dávid was taken aback that his sister would refuse to have any of the servants take her burden from her. The satchels she and Ambrus carried contained items they'd bring back to the reliquary room, in fact, but Dávid was never privy to what those items were, and by the time he was able to catch up to the pair, they'd already have their things locked up in some of the old containers in that strange room.

Someday, he kept telling himself. Someday he'd be allowed to be involved in the family business or at the very least, allowed some inside information.

Youth being youth, however, Dávid's disappointment was easily subdued by other things, and his attention would be turned down a wholly different road. His studies took precedence, of course, but equal in importance was his letter-writing to Lóránt. And as the seasons changed, he was also brought outdoors for a good deal of exercise and exploration in the company of his fathers, no matter the state of the wood and mountains, no matter the temperatures, no matter the weather.

It also didn't matter if the day—a week after his family's return—also happened to be his eighteenth birthday, which Dávid had been waiting for with growing impatience. A family feast was planned, and the servants scurried around to prepare the house for upcoming festivities—so much trouble, Dávid thought with great delight, for him. At least he was able to keep his mind on his work throughout the morning in his tutor's company, and when the hour drew close to noon, Mr. Szarka withdrew, claiming it was Apa and Pa's wish that Dávid's lessons would be cut short on his birthday. And Dávid simply relished the special attention, of course.

That day was cold and foggy, the recent rains leaving the rough country road running past their house a muddy wreck. And Dávid would have happily stuck around the house and played with Piri and Matild in front of the brightly lit fireplace in the drawing-room had Apa not ordered him to bundle up for a walk.

"But it's cold out there, Apa," he protested, peering out the window and screwing his face at the sluggishly rolling fog outside. The sun might be up, but its rays barely pierced the gray-white shroud, leaving trees and rocks swathed in spectral bandages.

"I'm afraid it's necessary. Ambrus and Éva had to endure this form of exercise when they were younger. Besides, you're eighteen now—finally, eh?—and this is one activity that's designed to help you develop your physical strength and endurance. Character, too."

Apa, clearly used to extreme conditions, appeared with only a thick coat and a pair of gloves on, his neck and head left uncovered. He grinned at a fretful Dávid, who nevertheless knew better than to push his luck and reluctantly threw on his coat, scarf, and gloves.

The pair were soon outside, moving through the fog and listening to birdsong lifting the gloomy air around them. Dávid, unsure if he were supposed to feel bemused by all this, certainly didn't expect to spend part of his birthday trudging through mud and fog.

"So," Apa said after a moment's companionable silence, "have you studied the books and journals in the reliquary room? I know Éva tried to steer you in that direction when you came home with us."

"A little, but most of them were written in other languages. I don't know Latin, Apa. I can't read French, either, but I know a little German. The stories are also a bit strange—fanciful and farfetched, I mean."

"It's all right, son. It's still good to read what you can. Your brother and sister had the same difficulties—Éva more so than Ambrus, actually, since the nuns who looked after her in that orphanage only taught her 'girl things' as your sister jokingly calls domestic activities." Apa shook his head, sighing heavily, but Dávid sensed no anger in him. Frustration, perhaps, but no anger. "So many years wasted for those poor girls. Anyway, Éva's been brought up to speed, of course, since she's been coming with us on our excursions."

Dávid glanced at his father. Excursions? He'd never heard these business trips referred to as excursions before.

"When do I get to go with you?" he asked. "Not the educational holiday trips, I mean, but business."

"Never. That is—if things go our way. Dávid, we chose you because we want a child to take care of in a normal capacity. Not be dragged into the family business because we already have your siblings properly trained to be our heirs."

Apa paused and considered, gazing around him and breathing in deeply.

"For so long we've been worried about the business and who'd be taking over, and, really, we only need two. And now that your brother and sister have proven themselves more than capable, it's high time Pa and I live like real fathers and raise you in a more—how shall I say it—mundane environment. Nothing out of the ordinary should touch your days, son. Nothing dangerous or terrifying. Nothing coming out of the darkest corners of the night—so to speak. Just school and perhaps university, eh? You'll be the first in the family to be a doctor, even. An artist. A scientist."

Dávid listened, frowning a little. What a really odd way of putting things. Confusion and disappointment gripped him, but he held his tongue all the same, suspecting his father wasn't quite done—and that there was a great deal more being left unspoken.

"That said, it's also good for you to learn more about the bloodline, and that's something you can find in the reliquary room. Read what you can, Dávid, and ask questions whenever you wish. Pa and I will gladly clear things up for you."

Here Apa paused again and reached out to rest a large but gentle hand on Dávid's shoulder without breaking his stride.

"We wish for nothing but a normal life for you, but there's no getting around some of the oddities that have been a significant part of the family's history, and it's best to be—forewarned, I suppose. Consider those journals something like your favorite boyhood adventure books but real. All too real, alas."

Chapter 9

If there was something that made Lóránt doubt his reality more than the strange night visits from some flying creature outside his tower bedroom, it would be the passage of time. His day-to-day activities might be strictly regimented, of course, with new ones gradually working their way into his schedule, but he never knew exactly what the clock said at any given point. And that was because there were no timepieces anywhere, and he marked the passing of the hours through the comings and goings of his tutor, his spiritual counselor, the servants, and the director.

The sun's movement across the sky and the moon's presence at night were his only natural markers, and even then, there was simply no way for him to know with any assurance.

A most pleasant dream-like haze defined his life in the northern tower as well, easily making the days pass in a way as to be something like comfortable, colorful streams of images. A deep and insatiable hunger for knowledge also devoured all awareness of the outside world, and it was a pretty common thing for Lóránt to emerge from time spent with his nose in a book, blinking confusedly at his surroundings and realizing it was already dark with the spelled candle lamps activated.

"Sometimes I wonder if the north tower is enchanted," he wrote. "I can't follow time anymore, and I don't even know what day, let alone what month, it is. Yet I never feel anything—not tedium, not boredom, no clear awareness of the minutes or hours. Each day simply passes, and I'm always caught in a lovely cloud of mental vagueness that never affects my learning. It's so strange, really, and it's only when I actively think about time that I'm left unsettled and even a bit fearful though I don't know why.

"I do get reminders of my birthday or what passes for it, anyway, since no one really knows the exact day when I was born. But the director takes care to have a modest feast put together for me to enjoy with whomever I wish to spend time with. Not that it matters, really, since it'll be either Mr. Eszes or Sr. Beáta. At least both of them have grown on me and vice versa and treat me like a cherished offspring. You can also see just how well my education's coming along with my much-improved vocabulary, ha-ha! Mr. Eszes said I have a gift for language, which is quite ironic seeing as how I was born mute.

"As for my age, I'm now sixteen (celebrated it today, in fact) and am expected to live in the tower for two more years before my patron comes around to take me home at last. But I'm now also allowed to leave St. Jerome's for daytime excursions with a chaperone but nowhere near your home, I'm afraid. I'm heartily glad we're at least able to write each other so frequently, Dávid. Perhaps once I'm gone from here, I'll be able to persuade my patron to allow me to visit you though I know you live so far from everyone, and we can officially catch up with each other. No doubt I won't recognize you if not for your ridiculous size and bulk."

The distant hooting of an owl drew Lóránt out of his letter-writing, and as always, he froze where he sat, startled and blinking as though waking up from an unexpected spell.

He gazed around him after a moment's confused hesitation, and he saw nothing but darkness outside and a familiar warm glow within, the spelled candle lamps cheerfully lit in their little alcoves. A charming touch to his tower bedroom which Lóránt hadn't given much thought about until recently, especially after being told the four windows of his room faced the four cardinal directions for whatever reason. In between each window a small alcove was carved into the stone, housing a spelled candle lamp that surely meant something though Lóránt never learned what.

These candle lamps stayed lit until a certain hour—of which he again didn't know—and the little flames would suddenly gutter and die, plunging the tower room in near total darkness. If Lóránt happened to be busy doing something when that happened, he'd find himself caught out and forced to go to bed.

And with the relentless passage of time came the creeping dread that had become his nightly reality for a while now. He didn't know exactly when the anomalous terror—distant and indefinable—had begun its inevitable grip on his mind, but he did know it had everything to do with what was outside his bedroom windows.

He turned sixteen that day, and for whatever reason, the dread that made his evenings a touch cold now completely shrouded him in icy horror. *Go to bed now. Quickly!*

Lóránt's breath stuttered as the voice in the back of his mind hissed its warning. He set his pen down next to the unfinished letter and nearly knocked his chair over in his haste to stand up. A quick wash at the washstand with cold water left him shivering and hating that brief and uncomfortable moment of stripping down to nothing before throwing on his nightshirt. He kept glancing at the windows and the darkness beyond, wondering if he was being watched even at that moment when it was still early for his strange night visitor.

No use wondering. Just go. And he did, pulling the covers up and over his head once he was safely tucked under the blankets. He didn't know when the candle lamps' flames flickered and died, but they did eventually, and the tower room was lost in a heavy darkness that felt both familiar and terrible to Lóránt.

Sleep evaded him that night with that indefinable horror growing tendrils that felt around for purchase, gripping firmly where they found a secure hold until Lóránt trembled under his cocoon of blankets. He allowed a small opening for air, and he tried to peer out of the little cavity and catch sight of his bedroom. As luck would have it, he faced one of the windows and the moonlit world beyond; there was no way for him to avoid the sight unless he burrowed further under the covers and suffocated himself.

He didn't realize till then that the fog would come about in spite of a clear day and night—even after the winter season—but it certainly did. One moment he was watching the crescent moon inching its way up the sky, and the next moment a sluggish fog rose in thin, tattered forms. It didn't fill the window with a thickening mass, thankfully, sharing space instead with the moon and the clear night sky, but it arrived with something.

The stealthy sound of movement against the round tower's walls warred with Lóránt's increasingly erratic breaths. He stared helplessly at the window with the dreadful awareness of something working its way from one aperture to another, apparently peering inside each time. Seeking, seeking.

It started its inspection at a different window and ended its activities at the one he was watching, nearly faint with fear. At each window it would pause, and Lóránt held his breath when he thought he heard it breathing raggedly and even painfully—as though clinging to the weathered stone demanded too much strength, but somehow Lóránt was convinced it wasn't the case.

When it finally reached the window directly in front of him, it appeared to grip the protruding sill and held itself steady that way, rising a little to look inside. It had a head—of that Lóránt was sure—its hair sparse and thin and appearing to float around its skull, judging from the silhouette it formed against the spectral fog that heralded its visit. And at that window it paused much longer than at the others, peering through the glass and nearly burning Lóránt with the intensity of its stare. Its breathing seemed to swell in volume until Lóránt was sure the pained gasps and wheezes filled the tower room with their awful noise.

There was something about the way it stayed so still for what felt like an excruciating hour that told Lóránt's panicked mind it knew he was awake, and it knew he was watching it as well from the safety of his cocoon. There was also something so bestial in its presence, an unnatural savagery that spoke of a danger that couldn't be so easily defined—and that danger, moreover, centered its existence on the terrified boy cowering under the blankets.

It was madness, to be sure, to be convinced somehow that he'd be the fixed point on which some nocturnal creature aimed its fierce and unwavering attention. And yet there he was, realizing it for a fact not in his head, but in a deeper and more primal corner of his soul.

The thing at the window sniffed the glass and then the air around it, peppering its efforts with its usual ghastly wheezes. When Lóránt thought he couldn't bear it anymore, the thing hissed a word—*Lóránt*—before ducking out of sight and scurrying off, its movements fading into the night and taking the fog with it. Then all was silent and still, the moon no longer visible but still gently illuminating the slumbering world with silver magic.

He didn't know how long he stayed that way, frozen in place, unwilling and unable to move, but the hooting of the owl again broke the dark spell, and Lóránt turned around to face another wall, still cocooned and trembling. He'd write all this down as an addition to his letter to Dávid, but the spelled candle lamps were out and wouldn't be triggered by his movements. He simply had no light to help, and it was torture lying in bed, unable to sleep right away, his mind sunk in pure terror and insistent in its replay of a horrible moment.

What on earth was that thing? How often did it come to the north tower? How many of its nocturnal visits was he able to sleep through? Did it watch him still? Lóránt was peripherally aware of it before, and it had been too easy dismissing it as nothing more than a recurring dream—no, recurring nightmare—brought on by the day's intensive activities or simply childish imagination. Lóránt was also naturally a deep sleeper as a child, and it was rare for him to be roused by sound or something else working from an inaccessible and more primal part of him.

How he wished Dávid were there.

No, anybody would do! Even one of the reserves or, heaven forbid, Bartó Csonka and his band of bullies would be far preferable than this terrible solitude. But that was all impossible, and Lóránt knew he was desperate and grasping at every flimsy thing he could think of. He forced himself to settle down and use the owl's nocturnal calls to soothe him back to normalcy. It worked at length, and Lóránt drifted off to sleep for what it was worth.

Because whatever sleep did manage to claim him was thin and brittle at best, filled with dark images and darker voices. Whispering voices, hissing voices, all forming his name in shapeless mouths that breathed with pained effort and called for him to come out and join the night.

The roses are fed. The roses are red and plump and no longer hungry. Pick them. They are for you and you alone. Do not listen to the whispers. The briars whisper and lie. Do not listen to the briars. Look at the roses. Take them and let them fill your room. They are yours and yours alone. Do not listen to the briars. They seek you.

Lóránt jerked awake and sat up in bed, eyes wide and unseeing, his ears filled with hissed words that dripped ice and malice. Once his vision cleared and he saw another bright, cloudless morning, he knew it was all a dream and told himself so over and over again though it did little to convince him.

Chapter 10

Dávid frowned at the letter, absentmindedly stroking his chin as he considered, worry gnawing away at him.

"It's back. It comes back every night now, and since I turned sixteen last year, I can't help but be too well aware of it. I'm terrified, Dávid, but I've got no one to talk to about it. I can't wait to leave this place," Lóránt said in his letter.

It was the most recent missive Dávid had received, and he didn't know just what to make of it, let alone feel about it. He dearly loved his friend—had felt nothing else for the poor, solitary thing, and if it were possible, the insurmountable distance between them seemed to have deepened that affection. Lóránt's overly frequent letters had become Dávid's favorite thing since his adoption.

"What's with that scowl, son?"

Dávid sighed and looked up from his writing-desk. Pa stood in the doorway, dressed for travel and staring keenly at him through his ever-thickening spectacles. "Another letter from Lóránt."

"Ah. Your little friend. How's he coming along?"

"I—don't know, actually. His letters worry me now—more and more with each one I receive from him. I don't know if something's amiss with him, health-wise, but his imagination's gotten out of hand, and I don't know how to sort him out." He waved the letter. "He's been talking about monsters in the night, crawling up and down the walls of his room and disturbing his sleep. Sometimes he has nightmares about them, and I'm afraid he won't be able to see what's real and what's not. His letters almost read like those old books in the reliquary room."

Pa blinked and walked closer to the desk. "Has he always been prone to fantasies? I think you said so before, but to what extent?"

"As a child, he was very colorful. We talked about following the river that runs past the orphanage and see where it'll take us. I really couldn't spend a lot of time with him since he was always being made to work for the kitchen mistress, but when I did, he was always so full of wild stories. I loved watching him tell me everything his imagination came up with, sometimes struggling with his hand signs because his body couldn't keep up with his mind." Dávid paused to laugh gently at the memory. "His imagination was unrivaled, Pa, and that was one of the many things I adored about him. He—Lóránt gave me joy and hope when I hated being there."

"I see." Pa nodded, startling Dávid with clear indications of an active interest in such a small matter that didn't even affect the family. "Well—tell you what. Let's go out, shake the academic dust off ourselves, and enjoy the day somewhere. Then we can talk some more about your sweet friend—hopefully with clearer heads."

"Is that why you're dressed up?"

"Indeed. Now come along. Go get dressed and be quick about it."

Apa had gone off with Éva and Ambrus after breakfast, and Dávid wasn't expected back in the workshop for another two days. He'd been forced to take a bit of time off because of exhaustion, and since he dove headlong into the business of frame-making, he'd turned into a "ghastly workaholic" as Apa would often complain, horror edging his words and manner. It didn't help that Dávid owned the workshop and was the master craftsman as well as the merchant who negotiated contracts and sold his work to universities, churches, and aristocratic households not just in the kingdom, but elsewhere in Europe.

Dávid did as he was told—at twenty-two not too old to be ordered around by his parents—and before long he and Pa were on their way to some bustling town well outside their usual day-to-day routes for business or pleasure. Corloveni hewed closer to the kingdom's agrarian roots, proving to everyone that the rise of industry and machinery in the face of a history deeply intertwined with the earth and ancient magic would never fully overcome the past. People thrived in Corloveni despite the humility of their trade compared to their more modernized peers and their embrace of soulless machines.

And the longer they stuck around, weaving in and out of colorful shops and watching locals go about their day, Dávid realized this was what he needed for his rest to bear proper fruit. Not just sequester himself in a large, dark home in the company of beloved pets and efficient servants, but remove himself entirely from an environment that was now familiar and comfortable and allow his mind to be engaged in a variety of ways.

It was also the best environment in which to discuss his anxiety on Lóránt's behalf.

"So young Lóránt has been living pretty much isolated from the rest of the children, you say?" Pa asked.

"They're following strict instructions from his patron, apparently. I reckon he's incredibly wealthy and influential and expects his word to be law."

"I see. And how does the boy cope with the isolation? It can't be easy on him, I'm sure, being alone save for his tutor and his spiritual counselor. Books and conversation can only take him so far. Trust me, I know."

Dávid chuckled and shoved his hands in his jacket pockets as he considered. "He's—uh—he's coped well enough. Lóránt's a gifted scholar, apparently, and is just hungry for knowledge, so he practically devours every book that's put in front of him. But you're right, Pa. The rest of his time is spent reading other books or practicing art or taking a stroll outside the tower but nothing more than those. He actually believes the tower itself might be enchanted since time seems to melt, and he feels like he's always caught in a dream. He describes moments when he suddenly becomes aware of the loss of time as something like waking up, and then he's—frightened for no reason."

Pa listened, glancing on occasion at Dávid with a look on his face that Dávid couldn't quite discern. Gravity? Worry? Alarm? It was difficult to tell since Pa would then turn away when Dávid met his gaze.

"Given the length of time required for Lóránt to stay in the tower for study and improvement and—protection—I wouldn't put it past the director to engage in some form of magic to ensure time doesn't pass so tediously for the prisoner."

"Prisoner?"

"No, sorry—student. I can't think of anything else to describe your friend, Dávid. Being stuck in a tower by himself for years makes me think of a prisoner, but I know that's unfair of me. We don't know anything about this patron of his and why the instructions are so specific and rigid."

"But what about the nightly visits, then? What do you think of them?"

Pa drew in a deep breath. "Without being there or without talking to Lóránt and probing him for more information, I honestly can't say. It's safe to think it's all in his head, but..."

Pa talked some more, but his voice melted into the background and vanished in the cacophony of movement around them as they made their way down one of the larger streets. Indeed, Dávid's attention was torn from his father because in his curious observation of the people around him, he spotted two figures idly talking while gesticulating at the window display of one of the small shops across the street. And for a moment time froze, caught in a vacuum of surprise as Dávid stared, drop-jawed.

"Lóránt?" he whispered, uncomprehending. "Lóránt!"

Then he was sprinting across the street before he knew what he was doing, barely even aware of the carts and horses as he dodged them. Angry shouts and curses followed in his wake, but none of those registered in his mind. His entire world had shrunk to the slim figure of a boy—almost a young gentleman now—lost in a lively conversation with a portly, dignified gentleman who held himself up with even more aristocratic pride than a king.

"Lóránt?" Dávid stammered, panting, once he reached the pair. Their conversation died at his entrance, and both turned to stare at him in surprise—the younger one more in shock as he still had his hands up, frozen in the middle of signing. "Lóránt, it's me. Holy hell, I can't believe it. It's your Dávid, remember?"

Lóránt had always worn his heart on his sleeve, which had made it easy for Dávid to know when the boy tried to hide important and unpleasant truths from him. And with so many years under his belt now, the shifting emotions lighting up gentle brown eyes left Dávid speechless, the sight too beautiful for words. Lóránt had grown quite tall thought still no higher than Dávid's shoulders, his slim build at least much more preferable to the painful thinness of his childhood. While still too pale no thanks to a hermit-like existence, Lóránt nevertheless appeared very healthy and properly maintained.

An awkward moment of stunned silence followed before Lóránt made the first move, and Dávid waited patiently for it. The young man inched forward—doubtful, shy—his gaze fixed on Dávid and unblinking. Dávid saw the moment when realization finally pierced the fog of disbelief, and Lóránt's eyes filled with tears.

"Dávid?" he signed. "It's really you, isn't it?"

Dávid nodded, his throat thick, and in another second, Lóránt's distance vanished, and Dávid's arms held his friend in a tight and desperate embrace. Both laughed giddily, Lóránt's tears dampening Dávid's shoulder, but Dávid didn't care. Wonder seized him at the feel of his dear, dear friend again, the feel of Lóránt's body against his own a strange and marvelous thing, and Dávid found he couldn't let go.

They stood in each other's arms for a good while as people moved around them. Dávid barely noted Lóránt's companion—possibly his tutor—moving away to stand at a discreet distance, and he didn't even know where Pa was. Only his friend mattered that moment, and as the cloud of euphoria gradually dissipated, Dávid grew aware of his incessant murmuring and whispering, his hand moving up and down Lóránt's back.

"I'm so sorry. I wish I could have come back to see you. I'm sorry I left you alone for so long."

Lóránt could only nod against his shoulder, and he gently pushed away to sign, but Dávid stopped him with his hands holding Lóránt's face. He needed to see his friend's face, really map this older version of the fairy-like creature he could only remember till then as a little boy. It was impulse at work—a fault of his, he'd admit, no different from what had driven his temper before, but Dávid preferred this manifestation much more.

"God, I missed you," he said again before kissing Lóránt emphatically on the lips. A chaste kiss, really, but one requiring a repeat for emphasis, so—a couple of tender kisses, then.

He barely took note of the look of shock on Lóránt's face when he finally released his friend so he could introduce him to Pa, who'd finally caught up with him in a flurry of irritated lectures about safety and being the death of his fathers and all that silly nonsense.

Chapter 11

That feeling of being helplessly caught in a bewildering web made of strange dreams was back, but rather than that associated dread and terror coming with it, Lóránt was shrouded in a euphoria he hadn't known in such a long time. Speechless joy and disbelief filled him with warmth at the sight of his beloved friend—who'd grown incredibly big over the years though Lóránt expected it. Everything about Dávid had always been big, in truth: heart, bones, smile, and perhaps temper if temper could be described thusly.

And what a finely dressed gentleman he now appeared to Lóránt! Twenty-two years old, a successful craftsman and merchant, and dearly, dearly loved by his family—a knowledge Lóránt had held close to his heart whenever he read Dávid's letters.

Then there was that—kiss. Lóránt's brain would have burst in his skull as it whipped around wildly, chasing after sensation and thought while reality eagerly flung itself into the turbulence with giddy abandon. It was all Lóránt could do to stand back and gape at his friend, who clearly wasn't aware of what he'd just done in full view of Mr. Eszes and the older gentleman who'd now joined them in a rush of red-faced irritation.

"For heaven's sake, Dávid," the man stammered. "How many horses and carts nearly ran you over? Don't ever do that again!"

And Dávid, being Dávid, didn't care. He tugged the man closer, his grin so wide and vibrant and full of joy. "Pa, this is my friend from St. Jerome's, Lóránt. The one and only! Lóránt, this is my father."

It took a handful of seconds for Mr. Gárdonyi to take Lóránt in—as though he weren't sure if Lóránt were real or not. The gaze he fixed Lóránt with was boldly assessing, and a peculiar little frown faintly darkened his features. Eventually he gathered himself, nudged his spectacles up his nose, and extended a hand.

"A pleasure to meet you, Lóránt," he said as they shook hands. Large and warm and fond, Mr. Gárdonyi's hand wrapped around his not only physically, but emotionally as well, and Lóránt knew Dávid was ridiculously lucky in being chosen by this gentleman to be his son. "We've heard so many things about you through your letters—well, what Dávid's willing to share."

"Thank you, sir. Oh—and this is my tutor, Mr. Eszes," Lóránt signed, aware of Dávid's unwavering attention on him, making him blush. Mr. Eszes stepped forward with such a dignified and regal air, and the two older men murmured restrained greetings and a handshake. "We're here for a day trip, which is also an educational one, really."

He grinned back at Dávid, whose expression seemed to have changed a little though the attention stayed just as resolutely fixed on him. Was he seeing something odd about Lóránt? Did Lóránt look strange to him now that they were spending some time together at long last? Was Dávid disappointed after all those years and all those letters? Lóránt started to feel around his face for telltale signs of dried food or dirt, the heat in his face growing with Dávid's eyes locked on him in such a maddeningly intense way. Surely his friend would tell him if something were wrong, wouldn't he?

The unexpectedly awkward moment and its accompanying pleasant buzz of conversation from Messrs. Eszes and Gárdonyi for its backdrop was suddenly shattered by the explosion of black feathers and the wild cawing of a crow.

With a startled gasp, Lóránt threw his arms up in protection, but the bird—an abnormally large specimen that seemed to have materialized from nowhere—appeared to be intent upon pecking and scratching away at Dávid. The young man yelped and cursed as he staggered away from the group, flailing and ducking as the monstrous bird came at him with an unearthly fury Lóránt had never seen before. It refused to ease its attack, looking as though it were possessed by some demonic entity.

There was also something terrifyingly different about the bird besides the size. Its feathers didn't gleam in the sun and looked dead and dull, those dropping to the ground appearing stiff and rough. And the bird's eyes were misshapen and milky, its cawing sounding more like inhuman shrieks now that Lóránt's full, panicked attention was on it.

Around them passersby cried out in alarm but drew away from the scene with only a couple of men attempting to step in, but Mr. Gárdonyi's shouts held everyone back.

"No!" he cried, waving his hands wildly. "No, stand back! This is beyond all of you!"

Lóránt stared, uncomprehending, at Mr. Gárdonyi, who then moved closer to Dávid and the crow.

"Let's go, Lóránt." Mr. Eszes's firm voice barely broke through the din.

"Damn it, get this thing off me! Pa! Pa!" Dávid howled, and Lóránt could spot scratches and fresh wounds on his friend's face in spite of Dávid's efforts at protecting himself.

"Vámpír!" Mr. Gárdonyi raised a hand, and Lóránt realized the gentleman must have just fished something out of his pocket and was now holding it—whatever it was—up, the object capturing the sun's light and reflecting it a hundredfold. *"Sáncte Míchael Archángele, defénde nos in proélio..."*

"Lóránt! Let's go! Now!"

The reflected light turned even brighter, colder, harsher—as though it drew on the father's exquisitely controlled rage and disgust at the thing attacking Dávid. And when Mr. Gárdonyi lunged forward and thrust his hand between the monster and Dávid, the crow screamed—like a human—beating its wings wildly and with a ghoulish fury that wasn't lost on Lóránt. More feathers flew out in all directions as it directed its attention to Mr. Gárdonyi, who now spoke a rapid string of Latin that Lóránt couldn't catch save for references to the undead and protection from such creatures.

What's happening? Dávid! Oh, no!

The crow's shrieks grew wilder and more unearthly, drawing even more terrified cries and shouts from the gathering crowd while Mr. Gárdonyi appeared to keep his supernatural calm throughout the ordeal. At least Dávid was now safe though terrified and—yes, furious, his hat now off his head, his hair unkempt, his face marred by the attack. But his attention was now fully on the unnatural, enormous thing filling the air with its dreadful noise and its slowly unraveling form while Dávid's father placed himself between the monster and his son.

Lóránt wanted to scream Dávid's name, wanted nothing more than to pull his friend away, but it was Lóránt who found himself in the circle of his tutor's arms with Mr. Eszes dragging him away from the scene. Lóránt struggled against his tutor's hold, the sounds bursting out of his mouth those same pathetic wheezes and gasps he'd always been ashamed of, but what else could he do? Short of punching his tutor and kicking and squirming wildly as though he were five and not seventeen, Lóránt nonetheless struggled mightily against Mr. Eszes, whose astonishing strength would have impressed Lóránt were this had been a wholly normal moment.

No, please! Let me go! I want to go to him! Dávid's hurt! Please!

Again and again, Lóránt's mental voice screamed, but Mr. Eszes kept shouting, "We have to go now! It isn't safe! Hurry!"

Lóránt only managed to catch sight of Mr. Gárdonyi's blazing object pour even more light out and at the writhing construct in the air before him. The crow's screams now sounded female—human female—before the monster burst in a ball of fire, burning feathers flying and then drifting harmlessly to the ground.

Then the crowd swallowed up the scene as Mr. Eszes's progress proved fierce and relentless though Lóránt continued to fight against his tutor's hold, voiceless protests and pleas a pitiful effort against the noise of dozens of voices raised in alarm and terror.

The world spun and whirled, color and light melting into each other while Lóránt numbly kept pace with his harried tutor, unable to move against the strong hold of Mr. Eszes's arm around his waist. Lóránt had never thought his stern and aristocratic tutor to hide such a strength, which seemed superhuman at that point, but they were clearly all riding a wave of energy that would likely leave them both drained and quite dead once inside the carriage.

Once they reached it, the coach driver flung the door open, and Lóránt was all but carried off his feet and thrown inside with him not knowing who did what to him. The carriage shook as Mr. Eszes followed, hollering orders to return to the orphanage immediately. Then they were on their way, and sure enough, a mere handful of seconds followed before a full body draining caught up with them, and Lóránt and his tutor slumped in their seats. Rumpled, clothes askew, faces fixed in expressions of confusion and disbelief, they exchanged glances with Mr. Eszes managing to recover much more quickly than Lóránt.

"Are you all right, young man?" the tutor asked, his voice again firm.

"I am, thank you," Lóránt signed after a brief hesitation. "A little frightened, but I'm all right."

Mr. Eszes nodded and sighed heavily, and Lóránt noticed the gentleman's hands trembling in spite of the return of his dignified calm as Mr. Eszes neatened his clothes. And when Lóránt's gaze drifted back to the man's face, he blinked in surprise.

"Sir, you're bleeding," he gestured, eyes widening. "Your nose, it's bleeding."

Mr. Eszes immediately felt his nose and chin. Judging from the lack of a startled reaction to this new development, it appeared as though the tutor expected such a horrible thing to happen. And it wasn't just a simple nosebleed, either, Lóránt saw—the blood didn't trickle out of the man's nostril in a thin line; instead, it must have poured out in a thicker stream, and it now soiled his mouth and chin. Mr. Eszes fumbled for a handkerchief and proceeded to clean himself with it.

"Nothing to worry about," he said after a moment. "It happens sometimes when I endure an intense moment like that one. I'll be all right—just need some rest."

Lóránt nodded and sank back in his seat, his thoughts flying back to Dávid and his father, his heart and mind lost in a sea of confusion and fear on his friend's account. What on earth had just happened, and why was Dávid suddenly attacked so specifically? Mr. Gárdonyi's brave interference and destruction of what had been obviously a chimera—what did he call the crow? A *vámpír*? What on earth was that about? No, Lóránt knew what a vampire was, but he never believed in such things, having only seen them referred to in his books of folklore. No, vampires were monsters of legend, and that was all, and perhaps he'd misheard.

Chapter 12

"There. Handsome and perfect as ever."

Dávid snorted but managed a little smile when Pa straightened and winked, holding the small porcelain bowl that contained the used towels and small vials of medicine. When he turned around to put things away, Dávid mulled over recent events, his thoughts torn between the memory of Lóránt and the incredible attack in the middle of a busy street.

"You know I'm not going to let up about this, Pa. You've been evasive about this vampire nonsense in the carriage, and I know—I *know*—Apa will be told everything behind my back." Dávid paused, scowling. "I reckon Ambrus and Éva will know as well. Yet here I am, the one specifically targeted in the attack, going about my day being stupid about the whole thing."

"Good lord, are you done yet?" Pa replied fondly as he continued cleaning up the family's medical supplies. Somewhere outside Pa's private study the familiar voices of servants broke through the silence of the great house. "Young people are so dramatic."

"Pa, I almost had my eyeballs pecked out. I earned the right to be dramatic. Now tell me, please."

Pa nodded and sighed, but he took his time with his task as though using that moment to choose the right words, which Dávid wished he didn't. Parents could really be troublesome that way, being overly protective even when they were dealing with an adult, and Dávid reminded himself not to be so hasty. He'd been successful over the years in controlling his fiery temper, but the need to lash out in angry protectiveness of a loved one still simmered beneath the pristine surface of gentlemanly breeding. And—and seeing Lóránt, now grown up and almost an official adult stirred that molten river, threatening an eruption on his friend's behalf.

Dávid blinked when he suddenly remembered the kiss. A kiss he'd thoughtlessly planted on Lóránt's mouth in full view of the world because he couldn't help himself—and had done it without Lóránt's consent.

"Oh, fuck my life," he muttered, rubbing his temples and screwing his eyes shut. How the hell would he go about this indignity in his next letter to Lóránt?

"That crow was a chimera—a monstrous construct—sent to come after you," Pa said, his voice breaking up Dávid's thoughts and momentarily holding back the mortification now brewing in him. "I don't know who was behind it or precisely *why* it came after you, but I will soon enough."

"What about vampires? Was it one? I thought those things are supposed to be revenants—undead monsters or something that, you know, exist only in books."

Pa snorted and moved back to sit in the armchair across from Dávid's. The look being leveled at Dávid was intense and troubled though nothing in Pa's behavior gave any of his anxiety away.

"They do exist, son. I—we—Apa and I—wanted to steer you away from the family's comings and goings because we wished for nothing more than to give you as normal a life as possible. Nothing like ours. Or Apa's ancestors." Pa paused then, looking pained. "Or your brother's and sister's."

Dávid stroked Matild's head when she sat next to his chair. "What do you mean? Ambrus and Éva? Is it this whole family business thing you're talking about?"

"Yes. They know everything—I mean about the vampires we've taught them to hunt. They've done everything as well and are incredibly good at it, but it has to stop with them, you see. Apa and I were obliged to reveal all to them and drag them into our secret world because we can't bear children to take over our work and found ourselves with our backs against the wall a few times. And before you think we adopted Ambrus and Éva just to train the next generation of hunters, I have to stop you there," Pa said, his voice growing a touch louder with the last part because Dávid had opened his mouth to protest, and Pa knew exactly what he was about to say.

A tense pause followed, with Dávid eventually breaking it with a pitiful little bleat. "Wait—did you say hunters?"

A grim smile formed on Pa's face. "Yes, hunters. Our bloodline is made up of hunters, and in the past, husbands and wives sired children onto whom they passed their knowledge and their skills. Then it was Apa's turn, but his nature dictated a different road, and we at first agreed to end this terrible calling with us, that this family's line of hunters will disappear with our deaths. We wanted children to nurture and love and provide with a good, safe, and normal home life. And for a time, we thought we were on the right path."

Dávid swallowed, suddenly realizing he'd held his breath. "What happened?"

"An outbreak of revenants in Pozsony. A plague of sorts. The call to hunt had eased over the years and made us think we and other hunters have managed to purge the land of this curse. But were we wrong there. Just when we'd finally settled down with Éva and began a fresh set of plans for the family, the infestation restarted. And the calls to hunt came more and more frequently so that it started to feel as though we were battling a hydra." Pa paused, his face again troubled. "Then Apa got really hurt in one of the hunts—almost had his eye torn out—and it took him a long while to recover from his injuries. We knew then that we weren't getting any younger, and we were slowing down while the plague seemed to swell. We knew then that we simply couldn't walk away and leave others to struggle, protecting the larger population from monsters."

The bisecting scar on Apa's face, Dávid thought, stunned. He'd never thought to ask about it, convinced it had been nothing since no one else made an issue of Apa's injury, and, really, he'd learned to admire the scar and regard it as a mark of greatness like the silly, thoughtless adolescent he'd been. Never in his wildest dreams had he considered it to be a result of a horrific calling that could have killed his father.

"And—and Ambrus and Éva were willing?"

"Of course. Took us by surprise, to be honest. Ambrus had already been aware of the threat, having lived in his orphanage long enough to hear whispered rumors. It didn't help when children started vanishing."

"And Éva?"

"She's a scholar, your sister. And it was through books she'd read illicitly as a child that planted the seeds in her head. She was shockingly calm and expectant when Apa and I had to sit her and Ambrus down to tell them all. But together, your brother and sister proved themselves exceedingly well, and I believe fighting alongside loved ones really helps fuel one's bravery," Pa said, the earlier tenseness easing into pride and adoration.

Dávid touched his face and found his skin no longer stung, and he felt smoothness where horrifyingly deep cuts had left their marks not too long ago. Even in healing Pa was quite skilled, marrying science with ancient magic—something Dávid knew his brother and sister doubtless had been obliged to learn as well.

"The books in the reliquary room—they're all about the hunters, yes?"

Pa nodded. "Accounts kept by those who chose to preserve their experiences for the benefit of future generations. But if you wish to learn techniques or instructions on how to destroy a vampire, you're in for a world of pain, Dávid. Each hunter's experience is unique to them—their skillset, the circumstances surrounding the vampire's presence, and even the time when they answered the call. Previous centuries were at a greater disadvantage, I'm afraid, but that's the nature of progress."

"Well, they didn't read like guidebooks, anyway," Dávid replied, screwing his face in annoyance and drawing an indulgent chuckle from Pa. "I found them dull, Pa, but more like lifeless fiction—like adventure stories, even, but without the charm. There wasn't anything in any of the books I could read that told me they were about real experiences, but they weren't written in ways to hold anyone's attention."

"Not your attention, at least. Oh, Dávid. It's imperative that you try harder now. You were attacked today, and we need to understand what was behind it all."

Dávid took a deep breath. "As long as Lóránt wasn't hurt. I'd take all the chimeras any day if it means Lóránt stays safe." He glanced up and met his father's curious gaze. "I'd do it again, you know. But—much better prepared, anyway."

"Ah—Lóránt's white knight, I see. He's lovely, Dávid, and I can see why you're so charmed. He's so, so fortunate to have you for a protector." Pa paused, thoughtfully gnawing his lip as he studied Dávid. "Think of him, then, when you train."

"Are you serious, Pa?" Dávid straightened up in his seat. "You'll train me? Do—do you think Apa will object?"

"Oh, he will. And he won't hold back, but he'll understand why my hand was forced in making this decision for both of us. Brace yourself for quite a bit of loud arguing when he comes home."

"You can tell him it's for my benefit, and I'm more than willing to be a part of these hunts. I know how to balance my daytime business with the 'family business.'" Dávid felt inordinately proud of himself for wording things so cleverly. "I'm quite good in a fight, you know," he appended, and Pa shook his head despairingly.

"I suppose I can also say it's for your Lóránt's benefit. That ought to convince him."

Dávid paused his bluster. "Lóránt's benefit? Pa, he wasn't attacked. I was."

"Yes, but the more I think about it, the more I suspect you were attacked *because* of your young friend, Dávid. And that concerns me a great deal. I hope I'm wrong in my initial suspicions, and I'm most likely going to be considering how little time I spent observing him today. That said, there's still that miniscule possibility that I'm right to worry for the boy, and believe me, a hunter shouldn't dismiss any doubts, no matter how small or indefinable for the time being. Now—are you hungry? I'll have a cold meal set up for us while we wait for the others to come back."

Dávid nodded vaguely, his thoughts enduring another whip around, settling this time on Lóránt. He needed to pull every letter his friend had written and study it—really study it—to see if Pa's concerns had any real basis. Perhaps Lóránt's rambling accounts of his dreams and odd experiences had something to tell him beyond the usual excuses of a colorful imagination fired up by the night.

And when Dávid's thoughts once again settled on that day's events, something Pa had said so casually earlier rose from the muck, and Dávid realized his father actually meant what he said despite his hasty and smooth correction: *prisoner.*

Chapter 13

The daytime excursions ended abruptly, and a cloud of renewed vigilance hung over Lóránt day and night. Mr. Eszes recovered from his ordeal, and now even he'd begun to receive letters, which Lóránt would catch him reading with oddly feverish zeal in between lessons.

"Aaahh. Yes. *Yes,*" the tutor would murmur, looking as though he were caught in the throes of spiritual ecstasy. "It will be an honor, sir. The greatest honor."

Sr. Beáta, moreover, appeared to be terrified and also began to receive letters, though in her case it was with a good deal of reluctance that she'd read them. Lóránt wasn't even sure, but he thought his spiritual advisor would turn deathly pale when a servant appeared bearing a missive for her. And when she took the letter, her gnarled hands would tremble while she murmured something—judging from the cadence of her distressed whispers, Lóránt knew it was a prayer. He also saw her clutching her beads whenever she appeared for her work.

The director's presence increased, her examination of Lóránt's progress now supplemented with a thorough inspection of his accommodations in the company of Mr. Gaál and Mr. Bokor, both assistants much older now but still just as intimidating in size and manner. The director herself appeared to have aged into a majesty peculiar to her, as though growing older actually slowed her progress toward infirmity and death. She was well-preserved, Lóránt thought in uneasy wonder whenever she came by to observe him. Pale and fixed, even, the increasing lines on her face looking more startlingly artificial and lending her stern, unsmiling features an inhuman quality.

"She must have stumbled across the fountain of youth, Dávid. I can't help but feel even more nervous than ever around her because—I don't know, but she feels quite *wrong,* and I can't explain why. Mr. Gaál and Mr. Bokor are growing older and certainly look the part, but never her," he wrote. "The rules are also a lot stricter now since that terrible day, and I hate it! I wanted so talk to you so badly, and now we'll never get the chance while I'm still here. I'm really hoping my patron will allow me to visit you. I don't know how he is, what his temper's like, and it terrifies me sometimes thinking about leaving St. Jerome's for a life with someone I've never met but who's ensured my care and improvement."

Lóránt paused and looked around him, taking careful note of the dying light outside and the ever-growing terror of the coming darkness. Setting his pen aside, he hurried over to each window and check the security of the latches. And as always, whenever he did that, he couldn't stop himself from peering through the glass and looking fearfully at the gathering and watchful shadows of the wood beyond the walls.

A firm knock on his door startled him out of his nervous observation. He turned around just as the door opened, and a servant stepped inside with a tray of that evening's sleep tonic and a glass of water. She set it down on his washstand without a word and promptly withdrew, drawing a sigh from Lóránt.

He didn't like taking the tonic, but his nightmares had increased considerably following the incident at Corloveni. His midnight visitor was growing more and more agitated as it skittered like a wild lizard outside, crawling around the walls and peering through the windows, all the while hissing and chirping and whispering Lóránt's name. Increasingly broken sleep meant a terrible day of lessons on the morrow, and the director was obliged to have Miss Fábián put together some sleep tonic which would be dispensed in carefully measured amounts every night.

If only such a tonic would have a calming daytime counterpart, Lóránt thought at times, grimacing after swallowing that evening's dose and following that with a few gulps of water. He hurried back to his desk to finish his letter to Dávid.

"Why haven't you written back? I know I tend to write too quickly without waiting for your response, but it's been weeks, and I've yet to hear from you."

Lóránt paused, dispirited. Was it the kiss? Was Dávid mortified by the kiss? No, surely he wouldn't remember it since it had been a completely thoughtless and impulsive move—just one of those quick things that would never register in a smart person's mind. But it certainly left an impression on Lóránt, and he couldn't forget it if he tried.

"If it was the kiss, I'm not angry, I swear. I know you didn't mean it, and I'm not offended. Really, I don't know why anyone would mean such a thing when it comes to me, anyway."

And somehow writing that made Lóránt feel just a touch ill and even more dispirited than ever, but he'd rather endure that than lose Dávid's friendship for good.

As before, time's edges blurred as the days passed, and the hours' progress felt more like an endless river leading him somewhere, the currents relentless as they pushed him forward and forced him into a future he still couldn't fathom. A dark enchantment—of that Lóránt was now certain, and it seemed to have gotten worse since his disastrous outing.

His eighteenth birthday was less than a week away, and preparations were already underway for his departure. Yet he could remember nothing of those days and weeks leading up to then—only the dreamy monotony of his lessons and his free time spent reading and writing, the crushing weight of his loneliness softened considerably by daydreams he already knew weren't his. Such was the way of enchantment, after all, that his mind outside the classroom walls would be kept busy with an unforgivingly insistent diet of fantasies though for the life of him, Lóránt could remember none of them.

All he did manage was cling to the dreadful feelings of hope in his breast—hope that echoed the magic web he'd been caught in since his move to the north tower. It was as darkly magical as his daily existence because it had no clear tether, no defined point on which it could be pinned. Just a taunting whisper of flowery promises, urging him to surrender when the time came and simply enjoy the lush garden of plump red roses awaiting him. *Do not heed the briars, for they lie. They always lie.*

"Dávid, I'm going to write you once I'm settled in. That way you'll have my address, and you can be assured I'll be at more liberty to receive your letters as well as visitors. I wish I'd have been able to go back to our river and contemplate it once more—one last time—because I haven't been allowed to go anywhere else, and for the life of me, I can't seem to remember much of how I've managed to engage my mind so as to keep myself from going mad. It's only now when I write you and I recall your face and our moments together that I'm able to feel like myself again, and it's a rare and precious thing to me. I cling to it with the desperation of a drowning man sometimes, and then another day dawns, and I remember nothing other than dreams. I feel like a stranger to myself."

At the conclusion of this, his final letter to Dávid, Lóránt set his pen aside and wept.

It was the morning of his eighteenth birthday, and all his clothes had been packed. He'd hidden the small wooden box containing Dávid's letters in his trunk earlier on. And as he dried his eyes, he tried to remember his years in St. Jerome's—the bullying, the uncomplaining service, the children whose names he never learned, and Miss Fábián, the only person besides Dávid who'd shown him compassion and kindness. Lóránt knew he wasn't going to miss the orphanage, but a sharp edge of unease still tainted this new chapter in his life, and he wished Dávid were there to cheer him up.

His lessons had concluded the previous day, but Mr. Eszes insisted upon seeing him one final time in the classroom.

"You're a most fortunate young man, Lóránt," the tutor said. "And it's been an incredible honor to be chosen for such a task, shaping your mind. Pray you don't disgrace me with slips in behavior. I won't be there to sort you out like I did before when I watched you nearly pollute yourself in full view of strangers. He was in a rage because of that, you know, and I was obliged to do what was required."

Lóránt listened, bewildered, but he didn't reply. His tutor's manner was as perfectly restrained and dignified as ever, but the light in his eyes was unfamiliar and manic. There was something like a wildness to his gaze, a distraction of mind Lóránt had never seen before—one that was now barely contained by the fussy precision of a learned gentleman. Surely Mr. Eszes was referring to the embarrassing kiss from Dávid, which led to the tutor dragging Lóránt away to the safety of the carriage, and Lóránt understood the man's dilemma.

"I promise to behave, sir," he signed at last. "I'm sorry for embarrassing you."

"Never mind that. All's well, and my work's done. What a fitting and glorious end!" Mr. Eszes said, smiling when he shook Lóránt's hand, blood trickling out of a nostril and creeping down his mouth and chin. He turned away to walk to one of the windows and gaze outside before Lóránt could alert him, and Lóránt had no choice but to withdraw, barely hearing "Glorious! Glorious!" being hissed as he left the room.

Sr. Beáta paid him a final visit in the late afternoon just as the sun was about to set, and the carriage was due to arrive to take Lóránt away. The old nun looked exhausted and wan, her eyes dull and her manner resigned.

"Here," she said, pressing a rosary and prayer book into Lóránt's hand and wrapping his fingers around both with her thin and cold fingers. "Remember your prayers. You'll find they're going to be necessary where you're headed," she said, rheumy eyes fixed despairingly on him. "Forgive me, child. He was most generous to the convent, and I thought—I thought it would be best if I were the one to offer myself, save the younger ones. I hope you found something of value in the time we spent together. My poor boy—so young, so pure, so full of promise. I'm so, so sorry to have brought this on you."

Sr. Beáta kissed Lóránt's hand and left with her head bowed.

Lóránt didn't know how long he stood there, gaping at the door, the enchantment in the north tower weaving its final mocking web around him until the moment a servant knocked, calling for him to come down. An hour? A handful of minutes? He blinked away the fog and hurried to his bed to gather his traveling jacket. He passed one of the windows and realized it was open, and he'd have ignored it had it not been a voiceless whisper urging him to look out. Lóránt walked to the window as a man in a trance, reluctant yet compelled, his heart beating a frenetic rhythm.

He pushed the casements open and looked out into the fading light, the eerie wood meeting his gaze. The shadows were deepening, but there was still a bit of dull light allowing him to catch sight of two silent forms gently swaying in the early evening breeze, their heads hidden by low branches, their feet clearly well above solid ground. One pair of legs wore a gentleman's trousers, and the other pair were covered in a nun's habit. The corpses hung from two different trees, marking the true end of Lóránt's time in the north tower.

Lóránt screamed, a long, agonized wail of silence greedily swallowed by the dark wood before him.

Chapter 14

"Still no word?" Apa asked in a low whisper.

"None. I've already written him so many letters, and still nothing. I'm dying inside, Apa. He's always been the one to chat, but ever since Corloveni..." Dávid swallowed, the familiar sick knot tightening in his stomach again. It had become a physical response in him now whenever he thought of Lóránt and the danger he faced.

He felt a firm and reassuring hand on his shoulder.

"He's alive, son. At least we know that—if the crows are to be believed. Ah, is this it?"

Dávid and Apa paused in the darkness, which among the ancient trees of the ageless wood surrounding St. Jerome's seemed—felt—darker than the night. Colder and heavier with the weight of centuries' worth of cyclical sacrifices of the otherworld's acolytes, willing or otherwise. Apa had read the nature of the wood upon their arrival, and it was a ghastly revelation but typical of wooded areas around suspected vampire haunts.

"It is. I suppose it's all right to risk a brighter light."

Dávid watched his father summon a swirling globe of fire the size of a man's fist—St. Michael's Eye, it was called, and it was one of the most basic but significant spells in a hunter's arsenal. Dávid had yet to master the ability, but at least he could boast a talent for offensive and defensive weaponry against the night world. He gripped the long knife, restlessly testing its weight as he followed his father through a cursed wood long soaked in blood.

The darkness fell away from the warrior angel's shared power, a wave of scattered groans and sighs filling the night air and silencing the more natural sounds of crickets and nocturnal animals. Dávid immediately scanned their surroundings and saw nothing other than old trees devoid of undergrowth, their roots sunk so deep into the earth it would take an apocalyptic event to tear them all out. A glance to the right showed the orphanage's stone walls, and farther in but still visible because of its proximity to the wall rose the north tower.

Dávid nearly tripped at the sight, that sick knot in his belly tightening once again at the dark windows of Lóránt's bedroom. "Where are you now, Lóránt?" he whispered.

Yes, a look out of the windows would have given Lóránt a clear view of the wood, and Dávid tried to remember some of his friend's complaints about the silent trees. He'd always been uneasy about them, Dávid thought grimly. Lóránt had learned to be absolutely terrified of the wood though he didn't know why, but Dávid had the benefit of his family's intensive knowledge and understood far more than his unfortunate friend.

Think of him when you train. Yes, Dávid thought, as Pa's fond words urged him on with much-needed courage. Yes, think of his Lóránt—it was *his* Lóránt now, Dávid thought with embarrassed pleasure—as well as all those lost children and adolescents the world didn't want. Many of whom had vanished into the night for no reason, never to be seen again. Dávid also learned of orphanages suffering from the occasional disappearances of their luckless charges, apparently with no real pattern emerging as to commonalities shared by the victims.

St. Jerome's was the largest and oldest in the kingdom, and it was the only one to have an unusually precise structure in terms of the architectural design of the orphanage as well as the hierarchy among the children. Dávid had suspected as much, growing up in such a place, but he'd always thought it to be nothing more than the institution's tradition, which the director was merely carrying on. Now that he was free of its influence and had his eyes opened to a larger and more horrifying world, Dávid's concern for Lóránt swelled to unbearable levels.

"I now suspect this orphanage to be a favored feeder," Apa said, breaking up Dávid's thoughts, his words making Dávid's blood run cold with their grotesque implications. "The so-called reserves. This tower. I must write to our favored archivists for more information about St. Jerome's. The Stasiuk family move around on occasion, but their work as archivists and hunters require it."

"Stasiuk? You mean—wait, were they from Warsaw?"

"Indeed. You know them, son?"

Dávid's heart lifted. "My good friend was adopted by the family—Irén. This is amazing! I—"

The words died in his throat as did the delight at the reminder of Irén because Apa stood frozen in grim silence before him, staring past the protective light of St. Michael's Eye and at the two bodies hanging by their necks. The night breeze had eased its force, but there was still enough of it to nudge the corpses and make them swing gently like macabre ornaments.

"Dear lord," Apa breathed while Dávid stared in drop-jawed horror at the sight.

A gray-haired gentleman and an old nun hung there, easily within sight of the north tower, and Dávid's stricken mind desperately hoped Lóránt didn't bear witness to this nightmarish sight. But the trees in the wood were widely spaced, distanced from each other to allow someone looking out of the tower windows to see what might be half-hidden easily enough. It was clearly a darker and more primordial influence that gave the wood abnormally heavier shadows when the night came.

"Apa, they'll be rising," Dávid said, his voice trembling. "Should we bury them in holy ground?"

"It's too late for that. They've sold their souls." Apa inhaled sharply. "Let's cut them down and—"

"Apa!" Dávid cried when the nun opened her eyes and looked at them.

Her pupils were a stark black in irises of white, the surrounding sclera, blood-red against a corpse's gray-white complexion. With her head angled abnormally to the side, her body hanging limp and unmoving from the rope, the sight would have driven anyone mad from terror, and Dávid had to depend on his father's voice to ground himself. *Think of Lóránt when you train.*

The nun merely stared at them in silence, and a quick look in the direction of the other corpse showed the same awful awakening and even more horrifying quiet. Both of them watched Dávid and Apa without a single sound made or even a single twitch anywhere on their bodies.

A ghastly impasse seemed to prevail, living mortals watching the undead expectantly with Apa whispering words of encouragement to Dávid. He'd been training the past year, yes, but he'd yet to dirty his hands in an actual confrontation while Ambrus and Éva had already gone to at least four hunts since Corloveni. This was Dávid's first step into the midnight world of hunters and vampires. His own breaths rattling as his heart thundered, he nevertheless managed to keep his wits about him and again tested the knife in his hand.

"Remember, Dávid—who they used to be? All that's gone—their humanity a thing of the past. They were bought, and whether or not they damned themselves willingly isn't our concern. What they are now *is*. Be ready."

Dávid swallowed when Apa held up a crucifix in one hand while gesturing with the other to pull in the guardian power of an angel prince, murmuring the hunter's invocation for protection. *En antíquus inimícus et homicída veheménter eréctus est...*

The nun and the gentleman twitched—a slight and barely visible movement that grew more pronounced and vicious with Apa's continued prayer. Dávid steadied himself and thought of Lóránt, recognizing the two revenants for the boy's tutor and spiritual advisor—two people in the unhappy youth's life who'd mattered while still alive. He recalled Lóránt's excited and joyful accounts of the day's lessons, of knowledge just devoured and absorbed with relish and gratitude.

Whatever the reason behind the tutor and the nun's decision to mortgage their souls to the darker world of the undead, none of it took away the gifts they'd blessed an affection-starved orphan with, and for that Dávid would be forever grateful to them. He prayed for their souls' forgiveness and final rest though it took some doing for him to separate their past selves from the things he was now watching with revulsion and horror.

Apa's prayer grew louder and more fervent, and the revenants writhed in their nooses, hissing and chittering now, and Dávid caught glimpses of fangs being bared as the pair struggled to free themselves. Their brains no longer functioning, everything they did was a product of a more bestial instinct, and their struggles came to nothing. Still held in place by the ropes, they nonetheless clawed away at the air to grab hold of Apa and Dávid with no success.

"Take the tutor, Dávid. May St. Michael protect you," Apa ordered as he conjured another ball of light to follow Dávid. "Move quickly."

And Dávid did, avoiding the struggle of rational thought against actual experience because nothing in this made any sense, but it was all too real. Logic and superstition collided that night, when before everything he knew about revenants until then had all been written accounts and oral tales. Even the collected hunters' tools in the reliquary room had always seemed so fantastical and impossible. Merely a gathering of macabre curiosities through the centuries, dark trophies amassed by a bloodline chosen specifically for a task using criteria no one knew.

But as Mr. Eszes—or what used to be Mr. Eszes—squirmed and flailed, hissing and staring at Dávid with unearthly hunger, Dávid realized just how little he really knew about the universe despite his success in the mundane world. He thought of Lóránt again, thought of this once-tutor and the patience and forbearance demonstrated toward a terrified child, and another wave of gratitude and pity swept over him, feeding his courage and steeling his nerves.

"For Lóránt's sake," he murmured as he lunged forward with his knife held high as taught, angled just so as he jumped and swung, cutting the rope and allowing the revenant to fall to the ground.

Dávid didn't wait another second all but threw himself onto the tutor, turning the knife in his hand and plunging the blade into the noose-covered neck. The revenant screeched, the harsh wheezing a twisted counterpart to Lóránt's breathy cries, and Dávid pulled the blade out, turned it again, and sliced the head off the shoulders. The knife was terrifyingly sharp and easily cut through muscle and bone as though eating through melted butter.

The revenant stopped its struggles, and Dávid dropped his knife to rifle through his heavy satchel and pulled out the mallet and the stake. He could barely hear anything else with the blood rushing in his ears at the moment, his heart thundering so wildly as though desperate to burst out of his chest. His shocked mind barely noted the nun's struggles somewhere behind him and the ghastly rhythms of Apa's mallet striking a stake. Dávid pressed the stake against the heart and swung—again and again and again, feeling the nauseating crunch of bone under the stake's deadly point as it was driven deeper and deeper until Dávid felt it strike the hard ground. With another mighty swing, he drove the stake into the earth, pinning Mr. Eszes's corpse to the soil.

And just like that, it was over. "May God have mercy on your soul," he whispered, bowing his head in exhaustion.

Chapter 15

Never in his life had Lóránt felt this terrified even as he knew he was finally free of the orphanage. It surely didn't help that the carriage's interior was fathomless black, the curtains covering the windows a deep red. His companion, heavily cloaked with his face swallowed by shadows, spoke not a word throughout their journey to the castle. Yes, Lóránt reminded himself dizzily, he was headed for the castle—the same one he'd been watching and admiring from the north tower window for years whenever the day was clear.

"You're now Count Boros's consort—a surprising choice, no doubt, but the reasons are sound, and he was most convincing. The contract was signed, the bargain struck, almost a decade ago in case you're wondering," the director had said at their final meeting in her office. Her manner was just as frighteningly chilly and calculating, any pleasure exuded likely nothing to do with Lóránt as a person but with Lóránt as chattel.

Consort? Lóránt watched her in uneasy silence as she poured herself more wine from the gem-encrusted bottle the count had given her by way of thanks, apparently. It was a similar odd-looking bottle Lóránt had seen so many years ago when he'd first laid eyes on Count Boros.

The director took a long drink, practically draining the goblet of its contents, and when she sat back and smiled contentedly at him, Lóránt thought he glimpsed two small fang-like teeth reveal themselves before vanishing again when she pressed her lips together. Her face was certainly well-preserved for nearly two decades' worth of familiarity to Lóránt, her aging clearly slowed and taking on an awful artificiality that made her look more and more unnatural and wrong.

"Do not disrespect us, Lóránt Kárpáthy. Though you no longer count as one of us, your past is still St. Jerome's, and everything you do reflects on this institution. And everything you do is no longer our concern but that of your spouse, so mind that. We won't be there to help you should you displease the count in any way."

Lóránt swallowed as his thoughts strayed back to that moment—the unsettling final conversation with a woman he'd known all his life but who'd suddenly taken on a transformation he was sure no one else had expected. Her assistants might be generously paid for their silence and loyal support, but Lóránt was certain servants had noticed but were too afraid to speak. And as he traveled in the ever-deepening night in the company of a nobleman he knew nothing about and yet to whom he was now forever tied, Lóránt's swelling panic threatened to undo him.

He fought for composure, depending frantically on memories of Dávid and his affection for his friend to ground him throughout this journey. By and large, his efforts seemed to work, and eventually his panic subsided to a restless hum, and Lóránt found himself exhausted enough to fall asleep in spite of the carriage's rough jarring.

The final thoughts filtering through his fogged mind were of his frantic and tearful revelation of Mr. Eszes and Sr. Beáta's deaths in the wood, which the director patiently took in with a half-smile. And all she'd said in response was "It was expected, and they'd agreed to it."

Lóránt woke up before the carriage reached its destination, and soon the vehicle slowed and stopped. He blinked and sat up, knuckling the remnants of an unsatisfying sleep from his eyes while all that time, Count Boros merely sat across from him, still and silent and watching him with a keen and penetrating gaze that could be felt in the hollow blackness of the carriage's interior.

The driver opened one door, and the count disembarked, holding a gloved hand out for Lóránt to take as he helped him get out of the carriage. Lóránt signed his thanks, to which Count Boros raised the hand he held to his lips and pressed a cold kiss on it.

"Now come," Count Boros said—the first words he spoke to Lóránt since his arrival at St. Jerome's that evening—and gently led him down a grassy drive toward the magnificent, sprawling structure that was now Lóránt's home. "So many people call this a castle or even a château, but it's really a manor house in the French troubadour style, which is all the rage nowadays. You'll discover that I'm a great traveler and have spent a good deal of time in France. In fact, it's one of my favorite destinations in the west. I hope this pleases you."

"It's beautiful in the dark," Lóránt signed, a bit abashed by the way Count Boros watched him communicate in nervous, stumbling gestures, the interest quite palpable in spite of the nobleman's still-hidden features. "No doubt it's stunning in the day."

"It's my pride and joy—the summit of my private achievements. At least for a time—until today, of course." He raised a hand and softly traced Lóránt's cheek with a finger.

Lóránt quailed a little at the bold flattery, his terror and confusion momentarily muted, but managed what he hoped was a bashful smile. "I'm fond of gardens."

"I expect nothing less. The rear of my property boasts a wilderness of roses. You're free to explore it, of course, but mind the briars. They grow like a fortress around the blooms, and the specific variety I grow here has the thickest canes and stems, the lushest and plumpest blooms in the deepest colors imaginable," the count said, again taking hold of Lóránt's hand and pressing another kiss onto it. "We don't want to injure these hands, do we?"

Lóránt could only shake his head as he tamped down his surging alarm once more.

The briars whisper, and they lie.

"Now let's get you settled in, darling. I know it's been quite a bit of a shock to find yourself in such a situation, but that's only normal. I've arranged a grand ball to honor our union, and I hope you'll take advantage of it to meet new friends."

They stood before the arched double doors a servant had thrown wide open in welcome to his master, the interior barely lit by spelled candelabra from what Lóránt managed to glimpse. Enormous stone round towers flanked the pair, narrow gothic windows gloomily staring down at them under conical spires whose points strained to touch the sky.

The count had paused there and made Lóránt turn to face him, and there Count Boros pulled the hood off his head. Lóránt stared at him in growing wonder and confusion, his mind furiously questioning his own reality because surely the nobleman ought to be much older than this. Count Boros was a very handsome man, to be sure—sharp, chiseled features unlined by years of traveling and living, dark eyes giving the impression of ageless knowledge and wisdom. He wore his wavy hair fashionably cut, his sideburns long and immaculately trimmed.

He ought to look more like a man in his early forties at the very least considering the length of time since they first met, Lóránt thought. But Count Boros appeared as a man in his early thirties at most though he certainly carried himself with the dignified bearing of a centuries-old monarch. As Lóránt struggled to comprehend, Count Boros grinned and reached out to gently massage the skin between Lóránt's brows.

"Now, now," the count purred. "No frowning and no scowling allowed. I can't have you ruin such a skin with ugly lines, darling. Consider your age, please. I'll have that and your beauty as perfectly preserved as possible."

"I'm sorry," Lóránt signed. "I'm just tired, I suppose."

"Of course. Let's have dinner first and then it's off to bed for you, yes? I tend to stay up late into the night—reading in the library or sorting out business in my private study—but I'll sleep in a separate room to avoid waking you when I retire. Does that sound good? Excellent."

And before Lóránt could respond to that, the count leaned down to kiss Lóránt on the mouth—almost like the kiss Dávid gave him though this one was decidedly more intimate and a great deal more assured. It lingered and insisted, and while Lóránt didn't know what to do next, Count Boros took care to lead, opening his lips and pressing his tongue against the seam of Lóránt's mouth and easily gaining entrance.

A very intimate kiss before the night world, one claimed by a man from his new husband. Lóránt's mouth was thoroughly explored, his tongue sliding against the count's awkwardly, and Lóránt's face burned from such a bold and possessive display from a man he barely knew.

But he'd heard of such marriages before, all done for convenience or a specific purpose, though he could think of no real reason as to why he of all people would be chosen for a nobleman's lifetime partner. Lóránt was nobody—a mute orphan who lived just a step above a drudge with no real future before him besides more kitchen work in someone's household once he grew too old for St. Jerome's.

When Count Boros released him, he moved down to press a series of fervent kisses on the side of Lóránt's neck just under his jaw, where he no doubt could feel the wild pulsing of Lóránt's blood coursing through the veins in his throat. Lóránt didn't even notice the count somehow undoing his tie and his shirt to expose his throat to this much attention, but he was certainly partly undressed for it—and in full view of the silent servant and coach driver.

"You're incredibly beautiful," Count Boros whispered against the now-damp skin of Lóránt's neck. "And so responsive. So quiet, above all—beautiful and quiet. I've chosen well."

He straightened up, again grinning, the brilliance of his pleasure doubling at the sight of Lóránt's deeply flushed face and the slack-mouthed look of shock and embarrassment. Gently he pressed Lóránt's chin to close his mouth before taking hold of Lóránt's hand once more to hook it around his bent arm.

"My poor, tired Lóránt," Count Boros murmured as he led him inside. "Let me feed you. No, don't touch your shirt. You're my husband now, and there's no need to stand on ceremony—or modesty."

And as the walls of the manor house swallowed him whole, Lóránt couldn't shake off the warring heat that had been roused by the kiss and the uneasy voice viciously whispering in the back of his mind. He fought the urge to button his shirt and get his tie sorted out and back into a proper bow, and when other servants appeared, standing as two lines of silent and solemn mannequins in black, Lóránt's mortification turned crippling at his shameless exposure.

Could they see anything on his throat? Were there marks left by his new husband's earlier hungry attention? None of the servants showed disdain or revulsion or even knowing little smirks—only blank, unreadable stares followed by reverential bows and curtsies as the count walked past them, Lóránt on his arm.

Lóránt stayed numbed and stunned until they were ascending the broad stairs in silence, and Dávid's face once again forced itself into the front of his mind—careless and playful and passionate and full of life. But there was no need for that anymore, Lóránt reminded himself as he swallowed thickly, now that he was with the count in a manner he was ill-prepared for, and he really should get used to this new reality. *Goodbye, Dávid.*

Chapter 16

The crows rent the early evening air with their wild cries as they descended up-on the mansion and flew in low, erratic circles around and around. They flew close to the upper windows and then expanded their spaces from each other and circled above the gables before dipping down yet again to fly closer to the windows and their fellow birds. This was a remarkable pattern that left Dávid watching in drop-jawed wonder outside, his fathers and siblings also standing and watching with him though quite scattered.

Between his family's behavior and the birds', Dávid reckoned they were all communicating with each other, the crows being the ones his fathers constant-ly referred to whenever spies were needed for important information. Both fa-thers as well as Ambrus and Éva stood still and appeared to listen as well as read the crows' intentional movements.

After several circles around the mansion—tight and low, wide and high, tight and low, etc.—the crows flew off together for their nightly roosting, their cawing fading in the distance until nothing was left but a calm silence and the gloaming with its gathering shadows.

"He was taken to Boros's château," Éva said when the family gathered close. "The procurer—the director—is now a hybrid."

"She won't last. Forget her," Apa said. His face a fixed mask, he considered their next step and led the group back indoors, his head bent in thought.

Dávid sidled up to Éva and whispered, "What does that mean? A hybrid?"

"It means she's an unnatural mix of mortal and vampire. She's being turned but not in the usual way—quite likely through drink since food can't be tainted by a vampire's blood. This method doesn't work the way she thinks it does—well, unless she *is* aware but doesn't care if it means buying her twice the time—if at all."

The director had never been like that—at least for as long as Dávid knew her, and Lóránt's innocent observations about her unchanged appearance turned into the first clue when Dávid went back and reread his friend's letters with a wholly changed perspective. The idea of the director turning—slowly and subtly and, according to Éva, painfully with an agonizing death coming sooner than later—meant greed for power and wealth.

No doubt Count Boros had been paying her handsomely to provide him with those unfortunate orphans with physical or mental disabilities. The reserves. Those children the world wouldn't touch or bring into their families with open hearts because they were born "defective". No one would miss them if they were to be taken to a monster's den.

And what did the count do to those children he'd acquired? Quite likely gorged himself on their blood, reduced them to lifeless husks after a time, and whether or not those unhappy wretches turned into vampires wasn't clear since it was solely up to the count to decide their ultimate fate. Master vampires had been known to leave corpses of victims out in the open for the sun to burn not to ash, but to a state beyond a revenant's ability to be reanimated. Mutilated and partially scorched bodies had been discovered all over Europe, which had been one of the hunters' favored methods of tracing vampire movements. Count Boros was old and powerful enough as a vampire not to care about discovery since he'd gotten quicker and cleverer in his escapes over time, leaving his monsters behind to be hunted.

Dávid had also learned that turned corpses kept close to their master as a hive and that there had only been a mere handful of master vampires spanning the centuries responsible for the infestations. Three had already been destroyed in the past century, and their "children", left vulnerable without their master's influence and protection, were forced to scatter, making them easy to dispatch in bloody hunts.

All of these he'd learned when he finally made himself focus and reread those dreadfully dull books and private accounts in the reliquary room. His family had helped as well, but they'd affectionately forced his hand and insisted that he made the effort to delve deeply into those old family annals. And as a reward, he was given a choice of hunting tools from the reliquary room, and he'd claimed an impressively deadly set used by an aging widow from three centuries ago.

"So what do we do next, Pa?" Ambrus asked once they gathered in the drawing-room, waiting for dinner to be called. "He's back, and it looks like his feeder list is growing."

Dávid shuddered at the idea of orphanages turning into a vampire's food source, but it made terrible sense. Ambrus's own accounts of the rumors running rampant at his own orphanage suggested the count had polished his methods of acquisition through the years. With St. Jerome's director willingly selling her soul for money and false immortality, Count Boros's machinery was now efficiently running on gears lubricated by the blood of innocents.

All those children taken away in the night, some of whom Dávid had witnessed being carried off—they'd been happy to leave a place that had been cruel to them. They'd been full of so much hope despite the prospects looking poor for them because of their "defects", and painful and bitter it might be, Dávid refused to forget his final sight of them in those fleeting moments of innocent joy as they scurried to the black coach. And all that time, too, the heavily cloaked man he'd believed to be a representative of some nobleman was actually Count Boros himself.

Now Lóránt was added to the blood-soaked list.

"I still say destroy her," Dávid said, fury churning in his belly. "Knock her hybrid head off her shoulders. I'll do it if no one else will. If we let her live until her condition destroys her, more orphans will be sold to the count. But we need to make sure to get more information from her about whatever contract she signed for Lóránt before we kill her."

"Dávid..." Apa replied with a long-suffering sigh.

"He has Lóránt! I can't just sit around and do nothing. I don't know how long he has left before that fucking monster fancies a nibble, Apa, and for all we know, he's already done it, and Lóránt's dead! No, maybe he's already a filthy vampire!"

"Are you finished yet? Calm down."

Dávid opened his mouth to retort, bristling at being talked to as though he were a child and not a man of twenty-two (soon to be twenty-three, he furiously thought)—and a successful craftsman and businessman to boot. But he couldn't help himself, not with memories of Lóránt—*his* Lóránt—surging in his head nearly all day, every day since Corloveni.

And the fact that the letters from St. Jerome's had abruptly stopped coming after that disastrous and too-brief reunion only fed the fear on his friend's behalf. Dávid even made a significant effort at writing to Lóránt just as frequently as the boy. But all that trouble had come to nothing, and with the full petulance and impatience of youth, Dávid believed he was slowly being driven mad.

"Tut, tut, Zsigmond," Pa cut in with a bemused little smile aimed at Dávid. "You can't just tell a young man in love to rein in his impulses when his beloved's in danger."

Dávid blinked. "What? *What?*"

"If I may interject, I think Dávid and I should go to the château for a quick reconnaissance," Éva piped up from her favorite chair, stroking a snoozing Piri on her lap. "Day would be fine and safe though perhaps dull, but it'll give us a chance to reach out to Lóránt since he's likely the only living mortal there and will be up and about when the rest of the household's—asleep."

"Day, yes," Dávid replied before any of his fathers could speak. "And then we return at night to finish them all off—save for Lóránt, of course."

"All right, but good luck getting to the count with a veritable army of vampires at his beck and call, little brother."

Dávid glared at Ambrus. "Who said you're not coming with me? I'll need all the help I can get, knowing what we're up against."

"You're barely trained. You wouldn't be able to handle more than one coming at you all at once."

"Then train me more until I get it right!"

"What about time, Ambrus?" Éva demanded, impatience now edging her words. "We don't have time to train Dávid properly. As long as we're both there to keep him safe, he can be unstoppable."

"Unstoppable and reckless," Ambrus countered. "We all know about the fistfights at the orphanage. He'll just dive right in and do everything he can to beat the living shit out of every revenant within arm's reach before staking it to kingdom come."

Dávid rolled his eyes as Éva and Ambrus carried on, arguing over such silly details as recklessness in a hunt when it was painfully obvious a person's life was at risk—no, *Lóránt's* life was at risk, the very thought of which fed too many dangerous ideas in Dávid's head.

Was he in love with his friend? He'd never even considered it before, but—that was a ridiculous claim, he told himself. Pa had always been the one to insist upon the true nature of his affection for a dear friend, and Dávid could only blame that kiss he'd stupidly given a startled Lóránt in full view of the public for such a misapprehension. If a chimera had come after him specifically, he deserved it for attempting such a bone-headed...

Dávid blinked. "Pa? The chimera that came after me?"

"Yes? What of it?"

"That was from Count Boros, wasn't it? How did he know what was happening to Lóránt at that moment?"

"The tutor, I'm guessing. He knew through the tutor who probably acted as a psychic conduit and who also likely conjured the chimera himself. Not because of any skill in magic or the arcane, but because he *was* a psychic conduit. Count Boros used the man's own energy to form a distraction so that Lóránt could be taken away from you."

Pa spread his hands in surrender.

"All conjecture, Dávid, based on what I know. Mr. Eszes is dead now, and we've nothing to back these theories up with. That said, it all makes sense if so. Count Boros is nothing if not determined to get what he wants—what he believes he deserves."

All the more reason for Dávid to play with the ideas in his head—new, dark, and dangerous ideas he expected none in his family would ever agree to.

Chapter 17

The dark enchantment hadn't stopped, Lóránt thought as he dragged a hand across his eyes, blinking rapidly to clear his sight and his mind. He was still daydreaming, but he also knew those fantasies seducing his brain into lethargic complacency weren't his. They were fed to him incessantly, ebbing and flowing over time—thankfully never keeping him in a tight grip all day, every day, but frequently enough for him to lose track of the hours just as he did in the north tower of the orphanage.

Really, he didn't know how many days had passed since his arrival at the manor house, and daytime made it all the more impossible to get answers because the place was always abandoned.

Count Boros as well as all of his servants couldn't be seen anywhere, and Lóránt searched whenever his mind cleared itself of fanciful shadows. His breakfast and lunch were always prepared and awaiting his pleasure, with breakfast served in his massive bedroom's antechamber. Lunch lay under cover in the dining-room. Notes were left everywhere in a graceful hand, instructing him to entertain himself with books, art, and the garden. *Mind the briars, my love. They are dangerous.*

Lóránt would have loved to have spent time in the garden, but at least for what could have been a full day after his arrival, he'd wiled away his hours lost in books in an incredibly expansive library filled with centuries-old volumes in just about every tongue.

That is, if only Lóránt's head wouldn't be so gripped by those fantasies that soothed and lulled with insidiously gentle voices and images. More often than not, he'd find himself emerging from an unplanned nap, the book he was supposed to be reading lying useless on the floor, his head pounding.

That grand ball took place almost immediately after Lóránt's arrival, and he didn't even know what was about to happen had it not been for a pale and silent servant coming by to help him dress. Lóránt, at first relieved at having someone close to his age around, tried to communicate in gestures, but the young man appeared not to know sign language and regarded Lóránt blankly. And perhaps it was a lingering effect of the dark influence gripping his mind on and off, but

Lóránt couldn't help but stare at the youth in confusion, wracking his brain over what was surely an impossible puzzle.

"Excuse me, but do I know you?" he signed again in spite of what he already knew. Sure enough, the servant only glanced at him and went back to his task, behaving as though Lóránt hadn't attempted to communicate anything. "I'm sorry," Lóránt pursued as certainty grew, his gestures a little frantic, "but I'm sure we've met before. Were you from the orphanage I came from, too?"

Nothing. With icy cold hands, the servant washed and dressed him with silent efficiency, and before long, Lóránt was staring at himself in a mirror, startled. He was impeccably dressed in a gorgeous suit of black, subtle patterns woven into the fabric only visible when barely revealed by candlelight. His hair had been trimmed the previous day by another silent servant—an older woman this time and no one he recognized—and Lóránt's skin prickled at the memory of having her cold, cold hands brushing his neck, temples, and scalp.

"Thank you," he signed again once he recovered from his surprise, but he realized he was alone in his room. He didn't even hear the young servant leave, let alone feel it, but at least the crushing weight of his loneliness was eased somewhat by this new puzzle of recognition. It was troublesome, to be sure, because it nagged at him and refused to give up its hold on his mind.

Count Boros himself came by to take him to the ball, smiling his pleasure at Lóránt dressed like an aristocrat. "Magnificent, Lóránt—you're simply magnificent," he said before kissing Lóránt soundly, again with a passion and fierce possessiveness that left Lóránt reeling and unsteady. "Now that you're settled in, I can't wait to make love to you," came the whisper against Lóránt's slack mouth before the count pulled away.

The celebrations were already underway in the ballroom, guests moving in graceful circles around and around to the accompaniment of what Count Boros called a quintet placed in one corner of the massive room. As with the rest of the manor house, the ballroom rose high with black walls lined with only a surprisingly few spelled sconces and broken up by those tall, narrow, arched windows peculiar to the structure's French troubadour design. Guests were all dressed in black—pale, blank faces topping richly tailored suits and gowns, unsmiling men and women dancing with each other to exquisite music.

Men wore fitted suits under jackets with flared skirts that grazed their knees, and women with thick skirts over what appeared to be narrower than usual hoops and cages as Lóránt understood ladies' fashion. The women also kept their hair untouched and loose, tumbling past their shoulders and making them look all the more fairy-like. Had it not been for everyone's unearthly complexions and fixed expressions, Lóránt would have marveled at the sight, convinced he was truly in the land of fairies.

Count Boros took his place in the midst of the revelers, and following a brief instruction on how to hold one's partner, he led Lóránt around in a waltz. Music, dim light, and the handsome visage of his husband cast yet another spell on Lóránt, whose anxiety melted easily enough as flattery rose and took its place, and he couldn't help but smile in answer at the intense and unwavering attention he was receiving.

His awkward efforts at dancing his first waltz didn't matter at all—not to him, not to his partner. Count Boros still held him close and secure, ensured his safety among the dancers, took great care of Lóránt from start to finish, and he was amply rewarded with Lóránt's smiles and silent bursts of laughter.

The dancing paused for dinner, which was held in the banquet room, where four rows of long tables were set parallel to each other while a smaller one stood on a dais at the far end. There the count led Lóránt, the pair of them holding court, almost, at that head table, on which was laid a splendid array of food. The dancers gathered at the other tables and waited for their hosts to begin eating. Lóránt, famished, watched as his husband did him the honor of putting food in his plate.

"I hope you enjoy your meal," Count Boros said under his breath, their conversation as private and intimate as it could get given the very public situation. "I myself planned your menu. They might be unfamiliar, but they're very good."

"Thank you," Lóránt signed, eyes nearly bulging at the sight of chicken *pörkölt* and dumplings, cabbage rolls, and bread. He gingerly took a few bites under the count's watchful but satisfied eye, and he glanced up after a moment to find every guest regarding him silently from their tables. At the count's signal—a graceful wave of a hand—they all turned to their own food, which was served in nothing else but dark bowls and goblets.

Fisherman's soup? *Gulyás?* That was all their guests were having, while Lóránt and Count Boros ate more filling dishes? Lóránt looked down at his meal and then glanced at his husband's. Yes, the count was having meat as well, but no vegetables, and the meat itself looked different from what Lóránt was having. It was roasted, but it was dark and looked rather unappetizing to Lóránt, served in a puddle of thick red sauce with no accompaniments save for a goblet.

Lóránt couldn't help but regard the count's plate with a shudder of horror without knowing why, but he remembered the director's words and promptly drew his attention back to his own dinner and ate. For his part, Count Boros didn't seem to notice his companion's troubled reaction to his meal and carried on with relish—and a second helping.

The dance continued afterward until the clock struck two, and Lóránt nearly stumbled in his husband's arms from exhaustion.

"Ah. Time to withdraw, then," Count Boros said as he led a dizzy Lóránt away while the ball kept going around them.

More fantasies crowded Lóránt's mind, dark and sensual and frenetic at times, aggressive in their persistence at being acknowledged, and Lóránt was simply too tired and confused to fight against their effects. Images he didn't recognize flitted one after another as he felt himself lowered on the bed, barely able to keep his mind on the way Count Boros's fingers undid buttons and laces while kissing every bit of flushed skin being exposed to his scrutiny.

The roses are red and plump and well-fed, ready for your attention.

Lips and tongue traced a wet path to Lóránt's mouth, and he was soon pinned under the count's weight, his mouth pried open and filled with his husband's restless tongue. Excitement and heat surged, burning their way through his body, pooling in his groin until he had to shift uncomfortably and spread his legs, realizing he was still fully clothed save for his exposed shoulders and neck.

"Rub against me, my love. There you go. Take your pleasure, and I'll take mine," the count murmured against his lips. And Lóránt, caught in the throes of spiraling excitement, rutted frantically against his husband's body, awkward and inarticulate, half-embarrassed by his ignorance and half-embarrassed by the fact that he was enjoying every delicious moment of friction. Lóránt wrapped his arms tightly around the count's shoulders, turning his face to expose his throat to his husband's hungry attentions while the count kissed and licked his way all over Lóránt's face and neck.

Was he going about this right? Surely the count understood his bumbling and stupid attempts at claiming his pleasure. He was nowhere near as soiled as Mr. Eszes had accused him to be, and the nearly forgotten kiss he'd enjoyed from Dávid almost ruined the pleasure being coaxed out of him. Lóránt's erection strained against his trousers, and he rubbed deliriously against Count Boros's front, his lips open and slack as ragged gasps blew past them. Given the way his husband appeared to relish their moment together, Lóránt wasn't soiled at all.

"My beautiful, delicious boy. Come for me," the count whispered, and something pointed lightly scraped Lóránt's throat.

Lóránt came then, spilling in his clothes, his eyes wide open and sightless and his mouth open in a wheezing cry while something pierced his throat and fixed itself there, two sharp points sinking into heated skin. A rhythmic sucking followed, and Lóránt was lost in icy pain and fiery pleasure as he ejaculated yet again, his body straining and struggling under the press of his husband's weight. *No more, please! No more!* he thought—unless that was yet another fanciful thing planted in his mind.

Weakened by his exertions and—and perhaps by the evening's activities—Lóránt slowly sank into oblivion, panting and baffled, familiar terror now edging his slipping consciousness. He tried to look at his husband when Count Boros raised himself up for a final kiss, but those cursed fancies again muddled his perceptions, making his husband's mouth appear stained with blood.

Chapter 18

Dávid had to admit, the château was ridiculously gorgeous viewed up close—and in the harsh light of day. Gray stone, black spires, a generous number of embellished windows in a variety of shapes loomed before him and Éva as they peered out from their cover (a great old oak close to the property's borders).

It was a majestic and immense structure, and Dávid tried to imagine Lóránt, who wasn't a particularly large boy to begin with, living in it with so much space around him. And to think, Lóránt would be alone in the day with the rest of the household hidden in their crypts, lost in the cursed sleep of the undead. A quick glance around the property outside revealed nothing much but grass and bushes properly maintained *just so,* enough to give off a hint of aristocratic neglect. No doubt the rear part of the grounds boasted the same.

"Let's go to the back," he said, nudging his sister with his elbow.

Éva nodded, her face fixed in an expression of intense concentration with a touch of doubt and confusion. She must be sensing something or reading something in Count Boros's property she couldn't quite put her finger on—at least Dávid hoped so, anyway. He could ill-afford to be kept from finding Lóránt, not knowing how well his unfortunate friend was faring with this bizarre change in circumstances.

They crept around the perimeter, keeping to the widely spaced trees surrounding the grounds until they reached the back. All was silent save for the usual sounds of nature around them, the château a mute, overly romanticized carcass celebrating a bygone era's excesses. The grounds in the back boasted a garden significantly less manicured than the front lawn but clearly one that followed a very specific plan. Wild roses littered the space with grassy paths randomly cutting through dense, chest-high clusters of the plants.

It would certainly be a romantic stroll from what Dávid could see had it not been for the strange thick stems growing around and among the lusciously vivid blooms. Those thorny stems appeared thick—perhaps far too thick to be normal—and they seemed to look more like tangles of brambles than actual parts of the rose plants they belonged to. For the roses—also incredibly large, richly colored, and fragrant—to survive in something like harsh captivity among such thorny armor surely meant some use of magic.

"Still no sign of Lóránt anywhere," Dávid said, impatience and worry thrumming through him. "I want to go in, Éva. I see no walls built around the property. It's like the count doesn't care about trespassers at all."

"Well—we can try, but have a care, Dávid. Something doesn't feel right."

"Everything about this isn't right. Let's go." Without another word to his sister, Dávid strode past the last line of trees and stepped onto the grass. The brilliance and warmth of the midday sun imbued him with courage and determination to find his lost friend, and without losing his pace, he set a course straight for one of the nearest windows. That is, until the whispers called out to him.

Dávid stopped and looked around, startled. Surely that was just the breeze, wasn't it? A glance at Éva, who was moving with a great deal more caution and suspicion, her eyes keen and alert and taking in her surroundings as only a hunter would, told Dávid he wasn't the only one being affected by their environment.

Come closer! We are here! Here! See us! He paused then, glancing quickly at the cluster of roses closest to him. He saw nothing but long, dangerous thorns and thick stems, fat, decadent blooms bursting out of impossible tangles and teasing him with invitations for a touch. *He feeds us. He is generous. We grow rich and lush from our food.*

Dávid thought he heard a hiss from the roses, and he shook his head and blinked several times, pressing the heels of his hands against his eyes to clear his head. The air in the garden smelled of roses and rot now that he was standing in the midst of it. *We are hungry. Feed us!* Another hiss followed, and Dávid was certain he heard it this time around, forcing him to take a startled step back from the plant.

He forced his attention away when he felt his hair stand on end, his skin prickling from that familiar feeling of being watched. His gaze drifted to the château and Dávid nearly swallowed his tongue at the sight of white faces peering out of the dark, shadowy windows, all staring blankly at him with milky, unblinking eyes. Their mouths might be invisible had it not been for the ghastly smudges of something dark randomly marking their lips and chins.

Dávid stared in horrified shock at the faces, but they were gone in another second as though they'd never been there to begin with. He immediately scanned the rest of the windows and found them just as heavily cloaked in shadows and realized he was hallucinating—just like the roses, he told himself as he drew a shaking hand across his brows to clear his head.

He spotted Éva already peering into one of the windows, frowning, before stumbling back a few paces with a look of utter confusion and disorientation on her face. She was also muttering and occasionally waving a hand as though swatting something only she could see.

A spell, Dávid realized just as another white face appeared in the window closest to him, this time pressing a hand against the glass. There was an air of mockery in the apparition, a bold effort at taunting him, daring him to do something. *Feed us! We are hungry!* Dávid spun with a startled gasp when his peripheral vision caught something moving, and he saw a bloodless face staring at him through the thorns and roses, the mouth curved and smiling while the stench of rot increased, overriding the fragrance of roses in full bloom.

"Éva! Let's go!" Dávid cried, and he stumbled toward his sister who met him halfway, her face twisted in a mix of horror and rage as she continued to fight invisible things while Dávid began seeing more and more of those awful, smiling faces emerging from the tangle of thorns and flowers around them.

Now and then, he felt his head clear, and nothing but a silent rose garden surrounded him. Then the black spell would sweep over him again and turn his world into a nightmare of fierce whispers and ghostly faces and the nauseating reek of human decay. Some of the rose bushes even shook a little as though things were moving in their midst, seeking escape.

They bolted down the grassy paths and raced each other back into the safety of the trees, their freedom from the dark hallucinations marked by cheery birdsong and the playful kiss of the midday breeze. Dávid and Éva paused a good distance from the château to catch their breaths and regain their composure.

"Well, now we have the reason for the property's open plan," Éva quipped as she tidied herself. "It's enchanted with a dark spell, and that might also be true indoors, I'm afraid."

She paused to regard Dávid grimly. "If my suspicions are correct, Dávid, your Lóránt's kept in his place by this spell, and he's living his days lost in fantasies designed to keep him complacent and meek. Unresisting. It's bad enough he was chosen for his muteness, which I believe was one of the reasons for Boros to pick him specifically for a consort—a silent spouse can't answer back, can he?"

"What does he want from Lóránt? He was a kitchen helper in St. Jerome's. He was nothing, treated like less than nothing because of his muteness. All right, granted he grew up in—in ways I didn't expect, but..."

Lóránt Kárpáthy was a beautiful boy, Dávid thought helplessly, and he blushed in spite of his recent escape from danger. Was Pa right all along? Had Dávid always been in love with his little friend, a tender affection in childhood turning into something else entirely over time—and even with their separation and only letters exchanged between them? Was the seed already there all those years ago, and this unique fondness he'd always felt toward this unpopular and friendless child came with complex layers bound to be revealed gradually as long as Dávid allowed it, opened himself to it?

"Stop overthinking things, you oaf," Éva said, and she tore him from his muddled thoughts with a sharp slap on his arm. "It's not a crime to be in love with your best friend."

"I have to get in there. I don't even know how he is right now, and it's been almost a week since Boros took him. Fuck me, Éva, has he been turned already?"

"I wish I knew for sure, and you know I'd never lie to you just to make you feel better."

No, indeed. Éva and Ambrus were nothing if not excruciatingly blunt in the best of times, but Dávid had learned to appreciate his siblings' nature.

"Is there a counter spell we can use? Or is there a way to break the spell at all?"

"There must be a workaround, but this is something well beyond anyone's abilities, Dávid. I have to warn you now. But our friends from Warsaw would know since lore and spells and all bookish things are their purview. Now come."

Éva took hold of Dávid's arm and led him gently away, still talking about the Stasiuk family and their incredibly deep knowledge of the occult and the darker, more terrifying corners of human history. Dávid would have felt some delight at the prospect of seeing Irén again, but his mind was now well and fully caught in Lóránt's net.

He thought about the sudden end to Lóránt's letters following their disastrous reunion at Corloveni, but he knew, deep down, his friend would have taken up his pen the first chance he got upon returning to the north tower. Lóránt would have written immediately, probably apologizing to Dávid for whatever imagined sin he'd somehow committed.

If the kiss Dávid had foolishly claimed from Lóránt affected the boy in some way, it was in Lóránt's guileless nature that he would blame himself for it and fully exonerate Dávid in the process. Dávid's heart ached at the thought of Lóránt assuming every mistake, which made the silence all the more suspicious. He himself had written immediately upon returning home, mortification guiding his pen as he apologized profusely for his behavior. Did Lóránt receive any of his letters?

Dávid's thoughts turned darker and more thunderous when they drifted to the only possible reason for this unexpected complication: the director.

Only she had full access to the orphanage's day-to-day activities, and if she'd become Count Boros's newest acolyte, she'd have paid particular attention to Lóránt's movements, possibly allow the same dark spell to be cast on the north tower to keep the poor boy complacent and meek until the time for him to be claimed by his "patron" arrived. Lóránt had complained about strange daydreams now and then in his letters as well as the puzzling loss of his ability to keep track of time.

"I have you now, you bitch," Dávid murmured, and he smiled grimly as new schemes formed. He'd be in so much trouble with his fathers, but he needed to do this. Someone had to, and no time should be spared.

Chapter 19

None of the clocks in the manor worked, Lóránt discovered quickly enough, and there were several of them. Gorgeously crafted grandfather clocks from Bavaria—another of Count Boros's favorite haunts—stood like dark, silent sentinels against black walls and stared out in grim disapproval at the sole living creature moving about in the day. Each clock also appeared to have stopped at a different time from its brethren, and had it not been for the sun and moon's movements outside, Lóránt truly wouldn't have known the approximate hour.

And, by God, he was so lonely, wandering from room to empty room after each meal, seeking his husband or even a servant or two for company or a quick conversation. He'd picked up his pen, of course, immediately writing to Dávid a couple of days—or somewhere thereabouts—following the ball.

"I miss you terribly. It's so lonely here with me being given everything I've never had at the orphanage save for companionship," he wrote, blinking away the tears and impatiently scrubbing them off his face when he failed to keep them in check. "I've never been so well-fed and given so many books to lose myself in. There's even a rose garden I'm expected to explore at my leisure, but I can't get myself to step outside. There are so many books and not enough time in the day, and there are so many rooms I'd love to look into. But I'm so dizzy just about all day, every day, and I wander around like someone caught in a dark dream.

"My mind's beset with so many strange and terrifying things, Dávid, and though I emerge from them as though I were just waking up from a brief nap, I don't know when the next wave of these daydreams (I'm not sure I should even call them that anymore) is going to sweep me away. There's neither rhyme nor reason for their movements; they simply happen, and I'm always caught unawares. In the evenings, for instance, I keep seeing a servant or two going about their work who look so familiar, and my instinct's insistent upon it. They never respond to me and simply look quite blank and stay silent, but I know, deep down, I've seen them before. I reckon they used to be from the orphanage, but I never get my answer.

"Save for the count, no one ever speaks, and for once, I'm not at all comforted by the fact that I'm not the only mute in this place. And that's because

I *know* they aren't. I'd ask my husband, but I keep forgetting because the moment he appears, my attention is fully on him and what we're doing to pass the time with, and I'm once again lost in strange fancies—stronger this time and far more vivid, and all I can do is to cling to him for reality."

Lóránt sat back and considered, his mind staying clear throughout his writing, and he chased after so many unspoken things. No, he told himself fiercely, palming his cheeks to dry the wetness left by his tears—no, he really ought to take advantage of the daytime hours to discover the manor's secrets. He'd be beset by those dreaded fancies again, but in between bouts, he should be looking for the servants and the count, who'd laughingly reassured Lóránt he was asleep in the day.

"My love, you're the only resident here who isn't a night owl," the count said with a playful twinkle in his eyes as they ate supper just the previous night—or was it the night before? "But that'll change soon enough. I'm ensuring it."

"But there's nothing to do at night—nothing to see. And how can you go out on explorations when it's dark outside?" he signed. His gaze dropped to his hands, and he vaguely noted just how pale they were. Really, he needed to spend more time in the sun, not in the moonlight.

"Don't let mortal limitations stifle your imagination. You'll discover what I mean when the time comes."

Mortal limitations? Mortal? The count punctuated his conversation with a wink before taking another bite out of the dreadful meat he seemed to eat just about every night, the thick red sauce included. The only other variation to his meals were the bowls of dark soup that Lóránt suspected their guests had also enjoyed the night of the ball while Lóránt's meals always varied and were quite wonderful.

Lóránt thought back to that moment and stood up, hurrying to his wardrobe to dig around for his little keepsake box. It contained Dávid's letters neatly bundled with a silk ribbon as well as the rosary and prayer book Sr. Beáta had given Lóránt. Both sat on top of Dávid's letters, and now that Lóránt was taking the time to look at them, he was astonished at what he was seeing—*really* seeing.

The rosary was a larger and heavier set, he discovered, the beads and cross made from wood that had been barely polished for use—quite likely handmade by someone from the same convent the unfortunate nun had come from. The slightly irregular finish and shape of the beads suggested a hasty creation as well, which only made the hair on Lóránt's skin stand on end. What did the nuns know, after all, about St. Jerome's in general and him in particular? Did Sr. Beáta say anything to them? At the very least, Lóránt was more reassured about the rosary being blessed prior to him receiving it.

He set it aside and picked up the prayer book, which didn't at all look like the ones used at the orphanage. This one was the same size and thickness, yes, but it was also significantly older and showed a great deal of use by previous owners. The pages were already discolored, the binding loosened in places, but nothing had torn off. The ink was also beginning to fade, the most surprising detail about the prayer book being its clearly handmade quality.

The prayers, all written on the right pages, were German from what Lóránt could discern, and the text was clearly the hand of a long-gone scribe. Black and red ink were primarily used, and an occasional decorative flourish or border—all hand-drawn—was in a mix of green, gold, and red. The text was also smudged from years of use, but what was written on all the left pages were more significant. They were all notes in a variety of hands, marking the importance of certain prayers for very particular use.

"This verse I prayed over my poor Roksana's grave today. May the coin I left under her tongue keep her body earthbound, her soul gathered by the angels above. The Lord give me strength while I keep my eyes and ears open for her unwanted return," one note said in elegantly rendered Polish. A single name—Hieronim—was signed below it.

Other similar, brief passages highlighting significant practices surrounding a loved one's death and burial filled the rest of the prayer book's left pages. They were all in a variety of languages, too, and all were of some indeterminate age given the poor condition of the ink used. Lóránt's skin prickled all over as he turned the pages, his eyes widening, his mind suddenly free of the shackles of the dreaded spell that had cursed his waking hours since his move to the north tower so many years ago.

There were no inserted notes anywhere from poor Sr. Beáta though Lóránt did wonder if the nun might have attempted to reach out to him in such a clandestine way.

No, he thought, frowning, and he turned the pages carefully back and forth at random points. *This is it. She wouldn't have needed specific notes. This prayer book must be the message.*

No, he corrected himself again—not the prayer book as a means of spiritual comfort and consolation, but the users' scribblings on the left pages. Scribblings that had overtaken the volume of the actual prayers' text. And from what Lóránt could gather, those were all notes on protection, destruction, and grief, the prayers only serving as sources of strength. Emotional strength. Mental courage. All in the face of a dark and grotesque reality.

His heart in his mouth, he gathered his box and its precious contents and scrambled to the window seat to take advantage of the late morning sunlight. There he read what he could translate of the previous users' writings, all of which seemed to be painfully private moments forced into the open for the benefit of whoever might inherit the book. And what was the most alarming realization of all was the recurring reference to one word: *vampire.*

Such things didn't exist, Lóránt had insisted whenever they emerged in conversations throughout his childhood and especially in Dávid's company. Truly, vampires had always been referred to in childish efforts at frightening him into good behavior, and none of the conversations—at least with Dávid—had been anything else but replete with laughter and colorful stories.

Was this what Sr. Beáta and Mr. Eszes had gotten themselves entangled with? Whether by active choice or reluctant agreement, did they sign their souls away for some reward after death? Mr. Eszes had behaved like a maddened zealot, and Sr. Beáta had confessed to offering herself up for the convent's benefit. A sacrifice. And the director knew—had always known—and had been an active part in Lóránt's unexpected change in living situations.

And now here he was, living alone in an ageless manor with too many rooms and too many secrets. Where were the servants and the count? They all slept, didn't they? Surely it would be easy enough for Lóránt to discover where. Surely it would be easy enough to disprove all those ridiculous and ungrateful suspicions now fermenting in his overly burdened mind, his imagination, sore and sensitive from so much unearthly interference, weakly firing itself up with suggestions of a household of the undead headed by a vampire nobleman.

The mere suggestion made Lóránt's stomach turn, threatening a full vomiting of that morning's breakfast. Even the prayer book had about it a sickly-sweet odor, half-fragrance and half-decay, that called to mind painted wooden statues in the orphanage's chapel so old that they'd soaked up the smell of paint, varnish, candle smoke, and desperate prayers from long-vanished years. Lóránt closed the prayer book and placed it back in the chest, but he held on to the rosary.

He glanced at the window again and took heart from the cheerful light gently flooding his bedroom. Without another moment wasted, he hurried out with the rosary tightly gripped, and he flew down the passageways of that floor, pausing at every door and opening it to peer inside. None of the rooms revealed anything to him, but there were still so many on just one floor with two more of the same above and one below, and the deeper into the maze of corridors he went, the farther he ventured to the rear end of the manor.

And the colder and darker the space grew. No spelled sconces were lit, naturally, for those only came alive when the sun set, and before long, Lóránt was standing nervously in the middle of a dark passageway with nothing but his stupidity for company.

He should have planned this better, not jump right into action, he thought bitterly, but when the dreaded sensation of another fantasy gathered subtle strength in his head, Lóránt knew better than to be caught in a dark spell in the middle of an ancient manor house's belly. He turned around and ran down the corridor just as the first wave of terrifying images emerged from the thickening fog in his mind, smiling with bloodied lips.

Chapter 20

Dávid paused for breath, for once wishing he weren't such a big-boned ox of a fellow because his bulk and weight made it ridiculously difficult to climb crumbling stone walls. He bent at the waist and rested his hands on his knees so he could settle his breathing. Somewhere in the distance, an owl hooted while closer around him, crickets kept their nocturnal symphony going. At length Dávid straightened up to take stock of his location, absent-mindedly adjusting the satchel hanging cross-body.

Ah, yes. He recognized the rear courtyard of St. Jerome's, unsurprised at the way the orphanage never changed one bit after nearly a decade since his adoption. In the bright moonlight, he saw the rough surface of the younger children's allotted play space and somewhere just off to the right, he recognized the door and the stone steps through which poor Lóránt used to come out of, his arms laden with soiled dishes. Those were the same steps where he'd taken a tumble all those years ago, and Dávid again felt a surge of grim satisfaction at the thought of him exacting vengeance on his little friend's behalf.

Now the bully had taken on a different form, and it was a far more dangerous one.

"Let's get this over with," he muttered, and he was about to move forward when the sound of crunching leaves as a heavy weight landed on them tore his attention quickly away from the building. He whipped around, his reflexes sharpened from several days of intense training, and he held a dagger in one hand before his brain could even catch up with his body's movements.

A large shadow moved toward him from the wall—the same wall he'd climbed just a moment ago.

"You're pretty damn fast for a trainee," a voice growled in the dark. To Dávid's dismay, his brother emerged from the gloom and ambled up to him with a highly disapproving frown on his face. "That ought to serve you in a hunt, I suppose, but it won't do just running off and leaving your backup behind."

"Backup? Is that what you're supposed to be? I need to do this alone, Ambrus! This is personal!" Dávid hissed.

"No one hunts alone, Dávid. You should know that by now. And I don't care if you're after a hybrid or a vampire—you never go about it alone." Ambrus paused for an answer, which came in the form of a narrow-eyed glare from Dávid. "For fuck's sake, I'll stand back and let you destroy her if it comes down to that."

"It *will* come down to that. For Lóránt. And for all those children she'd sold to Boros and whichever unholy thing of the night masquerades as human when looking for food," Dávid retorted as he hurried across the courtyard, Ambrus in tow. "Like I said, this is personal."

"All hunts are personal."

"And stop philosophizing on a hunt! I'm trying to think!"

Dávid's mortification at being chaperoned by his older brother wavered at the reminder of his going about this without a plan. Yes, he wished to confront the director, force the truth out of her, and then destroy her. But—how? He'd rather die than have his bone-headed attempt at a first solo hunt (if one were to call it that) revealed to Ambrus, who was such a skilled vampire hunter with a success record rivaling Apa's.

No—he'd have to read the room, so to speak, once he was in the director's company, and he'd have to use his wits as things happened. Absolutely no forethought would be involved, for better or for worse, but thinking on his feet had been a skill honed over the years in such a rough environment as St. Jerome's. For better or for worse.

The director's office was on the side of the rear courtyard, and Dávid knew which window to approach. There were no curtains, and the empty room was lit by a single candle lamp. There was no sign of the director anywhere, but that meant nothing since she could very well have just stepped out. And being a hybrid, she was likely turning into a nocturnal creature, which made Dávid wonder just how she was able to run the orphanage in the day—perhaps through her assistants if they were still there.

He made quick work of entering the office through the window. That is, he covered his hand with a strip of thick cloth and punched the old glass, wincing at the loud shattering when his fist went through—as well as a healthy shot of pain from the violence. A few more punches, and he'd widened the hole enough to stick his arm through, maneuver awkwardly until he was able to grip the latch, and pull.

"Someone ought to show you how to pick locks or even window latches from outside," Ambrus said, sounding unimpressed.

"I got us in. That's all that matters." Dávid pulled one casement out and clambered through the opening, this time not minding the crunch of shattered glass under his shoes when he hopped down. Ambrus followed as well just as Dávid surged forward, his gaze now actively roving about the room, taking in its contents. It should be somewhere—ah, there it was!

He hurried to one of the bookcases nearby, where half a dozen gem-encrusted bottles sat. Quickly he took each and weighed it, shaking the bottle to determine its fullness, and discovered all but one were empty. With a grimace of disgust, he also found the last bottle to be around half full, his vision nearly going red at the reminder of the contents and their significance. Of all the innocent blood that had been shed for the foul liquid they contained now that he knew and understood the nature not only of vampires, but their mortal protectors and acolytes.

How many others were out there who worked like the director? How many had died horrifically from their greed and unrepentant butchering of children, only to be replaced by others? Dávid had learned how hybrids ultimately destroyed themselves from gorging on tainted wine—wine that was really a watered-down version of a master vampire's blood when a true turning from mortal to undead before death required a vile combination of a vampire's bite and the ingestion of their blood.

Shortcuts were a recipe for disaster, but clearly people like the director desired gaining the result without putting in the effort. Dávid couldn't believe just how impossibly gullible and stupid people could be. Again keeping all those lost children and Lóránt in mind, he searched his satchel for his vial, unstopped it, and emptied its contents into the wine bottle, swishing the bottle gently to ensure the full mixing of disparate ingredients. He saw a faint mist starting to form from the reaction and re-corked the bottle and put it back on the shelf.

"She's coming," Ambrus whispered as he made for the window, but Dávid stopped him.

"I want to be here. I have to know," he said.

This time he couldn't keep his distress from making itself heard, and his voice faltered as tears threatened to choke him. All those lives, he kept thinking, the last one he'd seen being the girl with the cleft palate hurrying out of the orphanage with her pitifully meager belongings—smiling and so, so happy to be chosen. He didn't even know her name, and now he never would.

He and Ambrus moved aside, standing opposite each other when the door opened, and the director stumbled in. Dávid already had his dagger out, finding comfort in its weight in spite of it being smaller than the knife he used on the undead. The old widow whose hunting tools were now his had boasted in her journal that this dagger had been thrice blessed and spelled, a protection prayer to St. Michael subtly carved into the blade.

"Ah—Dávid Bodnár and guest," the director rasped, her voice gravelly and as unnatural as her appearance.

She paused only long enough to stare imperiously at them both before hobbling toward her desk, her movements jerky and marionette-like, indicative of the decomposition already happening inside her—as expected. Her outward appearance was ghastly, her white skin looking overly smooth and tight as though it were shrinking around bones and muscle, pulled taut with every passing day as a result of an unnatural diet of wine and blood.

Dávid shrank back, utterly repulsed, while Ambrus merely watched her in stony silence.

"Why?" Dávid finally demanded, horrified at how much his voice sounded almost child-like. So many of them, betrayed. So many.

"You ought to know why. You're a hunter, and hunters know *everything*, don't they? Yes, you're one of them now. You reek of it." She snorted. "Believe this—I'm not the first, and I won't be the last. This is so much bigger than you."

She made for the bottle Dávid had just adulterated, uncorked it, and drank directly from the vessel. It shouldn't take too long given her condition, which turned out to be far more advanced than Dávid expected. Such was the way of greed and the complete disregard of human life, particularly those deemed to be beneath her that she'd be imbibing without pause—an addict bent on destroying herself all for the cursed touch of immortality and the wealth that came with centuries of living and amassing.

"All those children you sold—how many?" he pursued, his voice rising.

"The numbers? I can't remember, but they should all be in my ledgers. How many of them have you destroyed in turn, Bodnár? They weren't yours to destroy. They were legitimately purchased. Ironic, though—the more you hunt, the more I'm obliged to replace. Justice works in mysterious ways, doesn't it?"

She tried to bark out a laugh, but the poison Dávid had managed to add to her wine was now burning its way through her ruined body—literally. She paused, confusion then realization followed by agony marking her doll-like visage in rapid succession. With a pained howl, she staggered toward him even as her insides melted, her flesh tightening further until holes tore here and there where skin was pulled beyond help. Bone and muscle revealed themselves just as she reached him, her corpse-like and clawed hands wrapping around his throat.

Wine, vampire blood, and now holy water—Dávid's poison—worked their dark magic on the director.

Her ghastly wails, mixed with Ambrus's cries for Dávid to destroy her once and for all came to an abrupt halt when the director violently jerked twice before collapsing in a smoking heap at Dávid's feet, two bolts sticking out of her back. He stared at the ruined corpse for a second in stunned silence, his dagger frozen in mid-air where he was about to plunge it into the director's neck.

He met Ambrus's shocked stare before turning his attention to the window and the figure of a cloaked Éva still holding up a small crossbow standing not too far outside. Silence reined for a second or two as the three stared at each other before Éva lowered her weapon and glared at her brothers.

"No one threatens my family," she said quietly, her voice masterful with confidence and disdain. To Dávid she added, "Take what you need and go. Quickly. We've much to learn from this."

Dávid didn't need another push. With Éva and Ambrus keeping watch, he hastily gathered the director's ledgers and Éva's bolts before leaving St. Jerome's forever.

Chapter 21

"I won't be away for long, darling," Count Boros murmured in between heated kisses all over Lóránt's face. "Just heard about some trouble happening at one of my places of business, and I need to look into it. Go on—keep it up. Yes, just like that. You're so damn beautiful, and—ah, yes, almost there."

He chuckled softly, forced Lóránt's head steady with his hands on both sides, and dipped down, his tongue dragging over Lóránt's teeth. What was so special about his teeth, anyway?

Lóránt was again pinned under his husband, rutting desperately against the count's still-clothed body while Lóránt lay utterly naked now. He'd already come once, but the count had been insistent upon the pair taking more pleasure from each other yet again. *We have all night, my sweet silence. All night. Soak my clothes if you wish. And I'll feast from you.* Was it Lóránt's drugged-like state, or did he actually hear the count breathe those words against his slack mouth and his now sore throat?

Are you turning me? Lóránt tried to mouth spite of his desperation for more friction and release. His arms couldn't move from Count Boros's shoulders, and his hands felt quite fixed, clawing into silk and wool for purchase. He couldn't sign his terrified question if his life depended on it—and it did.

His husband, at times a misty figure hovering above him whenever another wave of unearthly fantasies swept through Lóránt's mind, grinned, white teeth breaking past red lips.

"Give me another week after my return, darling, and we'll be traveling together. I'll take you to my ancestral seat, show you off to my friends—only a few left, alas. Then you'll meet others like you as well. 'Boros, how much longer must we wait for your turn?' they always ask, and we all have a good laugh at my expense. But they've no idea how particular I am, how patient. How willing I am to bide my time until the purest mix of innocence, beauty, and silence comes my way. And now look at me, here with you at last. At *last.*"

The count went for Lóránt's throat again, and more icy pain and pleasure tore through Lóránt's body. He stiffened and spasmed as he pressed tightly against his husband's clothed form, more seed spurting between them, and all Lóránt's exhausted mind could think was *Please help me! Someone, please!*

His body was utterly drained of strength, his throat felt on fire, and he didn't realize he'd begun to weep just as the count released him with a satisfied sigh. Lóránt blinked away the haze and the tears, and his vision filled with Count Boros's unnaturally pale and youthful face grinning down at him—cold and pleased, lips stained with blood. He pressed Lóránt's mouth open with gentle fingers and ran a thumb across the upper teeth's biting surface.

"So close. So close," the count whispered. "Then I'll feed you in turn, my sweet silence. But for now, sleep. And I'll see you when I return."

He moved his hand to press Lóránt's eyelids close, and Lóránt immediately sank into the dark waters of sleep. Whether or not dreams or nightmares filled the void, he couldn't remember upon waking up in the morning, but one thing he was certain of was the weakness and the lethargy that kept him in their grip.

Moreover, when Lóránt moved his gaze to his windows, he thought the sun was higher than usual, which meant he'd overslept. But at least his head was clear this time, and when he forced himself to sit up, grimacing at the crusted semen peppering his stomach, he also realized his hearing was a little more acute than before. Birdsong outside seemed a touch louder and clearer, the silence of the manor even more hollow and sepulchral.

Lóránt went about his morning ablutions and soon stood before the mirror on his washstand, combing his hair in place. He tutted as he tried to wipe the glass surface, but to no avail. His reflection appeared a little fuzzier than before, and he needed to squint just to groom himself. Then he froze at the reminder, and he set his comb down to unbutton his shirt and expose his throat—were there marks on the skin? He leaned closer to look, but the slight blurriness of his reflection prevented a more thorough assessment. He lightly ran a finger over and hissed when his throat burned all over again.

Any wound that had been there just last night had likely dried since no blood appeared on his fingertips.

He then felt his teeth but found nothing unusual. Then again, how did vampires use their teeth—their fangs? Biting their victims, yes, but did their fangs emerge only at that moment while hiding as ordinary teeth in between feedings? Lóránt's terror and despair reached such heights as to render him numb now, a glance at everything else reflected in the mirror only confirming what he already knew but couldn't—wouldn't—accept.

He was being turned. Slowly. Methodically. Count Boros was turning him into an eternal mate of some kind, a creature between what legends called master vampires and their "children". Lóránt still didn't know anything else about the undead other than what fireside tales had taught him, and he doubted if the library housed any anti-vampire literature. But of this he was sure: the furnishings reflected in the mirror were crystal-clear while he had his edges smudged a little, his overly pale skin now appearing quite unnatural. And when he forced himself to eat his breakfast, he wondered how much longer before he found ordinary mortal fare to be inedible.

Keep your wits about you, he thought when another wave of terrified tears threatened to undo him. He shook it off with an angry curse and scrambled for his rosary and prayer book. Another look out the window revealed the late morning, probably even noon, which indicated a gradual shifting of Lóránt's sleep cycle to a nocturnal one. It wouldn't be long before he'd be waking up at sundown and be normally tended to by an army of silent servants—many of them he was now sure he'd seen at the orphanage years ago.

How on earth did they end up here? He'd heard about reserves being taken away for work in aristocratic households. Was this the actual household being whispered among the rest of the wretched lot? Was this their ultimate fate—and with the director's active participation in their placement? So many questions, so little time.

Lóránt nearly tore his bedroom apart in search of what he understood to be tools meant to destroy vampires. Stakes were the most effective, he reminded himself, his mind hearkening back to those childhood stories—and daggers if he were to fail in finding something he could use as a stake. No, a dagger would be better for him since he didn't think he was strong enough to drive a stake through a revenant's chest. A long knife would be good enough to cut off a vampire's head, wouldn't it?

His heart in his throat, Lóránt hurried out of his bedroom and down the grand staircase, taking a dark passageway toward the rear of the manor where the kitchen was. It was easy enough to find, relief flooding him upon seeing it cold and abandoned. He found a long knife he could use, and on his way out, he spotted a few ordinary candle lamps and matches standing on a table awaiting use. He took one and promptly lit it. Another sweeping gaze around the kitchen for possible weapons he could use revealed a large, discolored key in a ring hanging from a hook over a stained counter.

Lóránt froze at the sight, his mind, oddly cleared of those dreadful drug-like fantasies, racing after thoughts that nearly drove him to his knees.

It must be a skeleton key that could open doors where the count's servants likely slept—perhaps even the count though he'd left for some business trip. Or so he'd said, Lóránt thought bitterly. Was Count Boros actually off on a hunt for food for himself? Clearly he required much more sustenance than just what he got from Lóránt, who was clearly there not for food, but for immortal companionship.

Nausea roiled Lóránt's belly at the reminder of his grotesque transformation, but he shook it off with another angry curse at himself. There was no room for weakness now—no room for hesitation or second thoughts. Logic no longer existed in this place, and Lóránt had to depend on myth and childhood tales to guide his steps if he wished to know the complete truth.

He took the key—a heavy, half-rusted thing—and went off in search of locked rooms. He found nothing of note on the ground floor and braced himself for the upper floors. Lóránt wandered some more until he found a door leading to the stairs up one of the round towers in the back. Terror of the unknown nearly made his knees lock as he ascended, but he forced himself to take advantage of his slightly sharper hearing to guide him, the possibility of his own fate should he succeed barely making an impression in his mind.

So he thought of Dávid for courage. Bright, strong, fiery, and affectionate Dávid, whose laughing visage and keen gaze were Lóránt's last images of him. He'd take those to his grave if need be, Lóránt thought, and when he came across the first shut door, he set the candle lamp down and tested the key, making sure to keep a tight grip on the knife he held in the other hand.

The tumblers moved with an agonizingly loud, rusty groan, and Lóránt took a deep and tremulous breath as he pushed the door open. He took the key out and reclaimed the candle lamp, and when he raised it up to chase off the shadows in the room, he nearly fell back in horror at the room's contents.

Old, weathered, and narrow coffins lay in haphazard piles in the chamber, with most lying on the floor while a few stood propped against the walls. Some of the coffins were seemingly placed randomly like macabre afterthoughts, some partly resting on others so that they lay tilted at awkward angles. Only two coffins still had their lids, and the rest exposed their dreadful sleepers, whom Lóránt recognized to be servants. And they all lay as they would as natural corpses—a deathly pallor combined with sunken skin and shrinking lips and eyeballs, their eyelids partially open, their overall appearance conveying varying stages of putrefaction.

Once the sun set, these corpses would reform and appear as the pale, silent creatures that were now familiar to him.

The stench nearly did Lóránt in, but he forced himself to walk toward the closest coffin. He recognized the body inside to be the one of the young man who'd helped him dress for the ball, and Lóránt knelt by the coffin and burst into tears. He remembered now—the boy was named Kelemen, and he'd been a jovial creature in spite of a bad stutter that made communication a daily nightmare in the face of mockery. Though he and Lóránt didn't move in the same circles, Lóránt still knew him in some ways, found he had so much more in common with Kelemen than he'd thought.

Do it. Do it for him. For them. Save them all.

A sudden madness must have seized him because Lóránt's mind seemed to retreat, his awareness shrinking to a smaller dot against a sea of shadows, and it was as though something else were moving his body and taking over.

He set the candle lamp aside and drove the knife into the corpse's neck, moving the blade in sickening ways until the head was completely detached from the torso, and rancid blood covered his hands. Someone sobbed, filling the tower room with wheezing gasps and tight, breathy whines. And with the sobbing came the awful sound of blade sinking into flesh and bone, of coffin lids being pushed open and of a few bodies sliding, headless, out of their upright containers.

Chapter 22

Apa was infuriated, naturally, but pride in Ambrus and Éva's participation rendered Dávid's recklessness more palatable and easier to swallow—with help from Pa and his marvelous skill in soothing with just the right healing mix of tea and herbs. Dávid withstood the embarrassment of being scolded within an inch of his life for a good fifteen minutes before being pulled into a tight and relieved embrace by a still fuming Apa afterward.

"Don't ever—*ever*—do something so foolish like that again, Dávid," Apa said, pressing their foreheads together. "It's galling, I understand, but you *must* accept you've got much work to do still to reach your brother and sister's level. Please listen. So many in my bloodline have lost children this way, and I flatly refuse to have that happen to us."

Dávid swallowed and nodded, guilt now taking over his initial sullen annoyance. Yes, once the fires were all burned out, he really did feel regret and misery for causing his fathers so much undue pain.

"I'm sorry, Apa. I am. I swear I'll do better," he replied in a quavering voice that made him sound almost childlike in his ears. It had been agony as well, waiting for his fathers to return from a brief trip—an extra day of excruciating anticipation following the midnight visit to St. Jerome's.

Apa smiled wryly and kissed Dávid's cheek, gave him another tight embrace that melted Dávid's heart further, and released him. "Now come. Lunch is ready, and we can talk some more about—"

Éva bursting through the study door cut Apa short, and her pale and grim countenance made them halt in their tracks.

"Apa," she said and pointed in the direction of the nearest window. "The crows are back. Something's happened at the château. Night's brewing over there."

They all but raced each other out of the house in time to find a murder of crows flying erratically all over, filling the air with wild and furious cawing. Dávid saw they didn't follow the mesmerizing pattern of communication they'd used before, and even Pa and Ambrus didn't stand still, mirroring the crows by pacing about in confusion while staring up at the restless birds.

"What is it?" Apa cried once he, Dávid, and Éva joined them. "What happened?"

"Another dark spell—the château. Night has fallen over it now, and there's a smaller cloud of darkness flying toward it. Something's afoot," Pa breathed, alarm clearly etched in his features. When he looked away from the shrieking crows, his gaze immediately settled on Dávid. "Your Lóránt's done something. The count's coming back to stop him, I reckon. The night spell doesn't get cast unless a master vampire's threatened."

Dávid didn't need further encouragement. The ledgers he'd stolen from the orphanage had yet to be perused in full, and the family was also expecting to meet with the Stasiuk family tomorrow for a discussion about dark enchantments and how best to break the spell that had been cast over poor Lóránt. But they'd taken too long to act, regardless of how little information they had. That had been the reason why he'd decided to take matters in his own hands with the director, and the failed visit to the château with Éva barely met with approval.

His fathers were painfully reluctant when Dávid was involved in hunts despite their agreement over the necessity of his being a part of the "family business". But Lóránt had taken care of that for them. Dávid knew there was simply no way he was going to just sit back and let his more experienced and far better skilled parents and siblings sort out all this nasty vampire business when Lóránt's life was in danger day after day.

And bless Apa and Pa, they also saw—too clearly—just how far Dávid was willing to go to save his friend. His dearest, sweetest Lóránt, whom Dávid was now determined to woo the proper way. And for that to happen, Lóránt would have to survive, any lingering effects of living with a master vampire and his servants completely purged with Lóránt recovering in peace and quiet and a healthy dose of joy and love from Dávid.

Armed with their tools and throwing on whatever spelled leather coats they could grab—used as hunters' armor, Dávid had learned—the family mounted horses and rode off in a cloud of dust. They followed the crows back to the château, their avian escorts and friends appearing like a small, wild storm cloud as well to anyone who'd glimpse them from afar.

The château not only stood in the mist-shrouded eastern mountains, but there were twenty leagues between it and Dávid's home, almost all of which were rolling terrain with an occasional grassy meadow here and there. Only one road linked it with the rest of the outside world, and even then, it was barely visible, being more of an unused and overgrown track now. They didn't know how long the count's cover of darkness had been streaking through space in unearthly fury, but Dávid desperately hoped they weren't too far behind.

Too late, of course, did he realize they'd yet to find an answer for the dark enchantment of the château's grounds. That had been one of the reasons they were going to meet the Stasiuk family the following day, the Stasiuks currently enmeshed in their own vampire hunt elsewhere. They were brilliant academics, yes, but they could hold their own in hunts with the help of magic—ancient and terrifying in its potency against the dark world. They would know how best to break the enchantment or at least override its effects. But now Dávid and his family would have to endure the horrible battery of hallucinations the moment they set foot on Count Boros's property.

He thought of Lóránt as his steed thundered across vast expanses and undulating ground, a creature carefully chosen and nurtured for hunts. He thought of the promise he'd made so many years ago, and he aimed to keep that promise. He was going to take his beloved Lóránt on a meandering journey on the moon-kissed river, heedless of their destination, their hearts simply awash in wonder and the simple joy of being carried by the gentle currents as Nature dictated. Such dreams and hopes buoyed his heart and fed his mind, his spirit hardening and bracing itself for a confrontation he knew he was still ill-prepared for, family or no family around him.

The crows suddenly broke their formation in what seemed like an explosion of wildly fluttering wings and black feathers raining down on the hunters. The birds flew in wide and scattered directions, circling around and reforming behind them, effectively leaving them for the rest of the journey, and it was easy to see why. The château lay directly ahead, a sprawling and lifeless structure now swathed in darkness as an abnormal block of deep night had taken over its property and the wood around it. It looked as though a cosmic giant had carved a hole out of the afternoon sky and forced the night through, in addition to which a sluggish ground mist had formed.

Dávid glanced up and saw no indication of the count's own progress toward the château, and his blood turned cold at the idea Lóránt was now trapped in the cursed structure with the vampire—alone and helpless. *I'm coming, sweetheart. I'm coming.*

They drew to a halt several yards before the edge of the night and left their horses among the sun-touched trees to rest and snack, and Dávid could feel the icy chill even from the safety of the sunlit world as they walked toward the château's grounds.

"Be wary of hallucinations. I had things coming at me, and Dávid heard voices in the briars," Éva said as she freed her modified hand crossbow from her hip and expertly wrapped the leather straps around her right forearm then loaded the first spelled bolt.

Along with the small, light crossbow she'd used on the director, this was specifically designed for her with Apa sparing no expense. The family required a clever, fast shooter who could incapacitate threats from a short distance so someone could deliver the killing blow. She'd taken up range weapons from one of Apa's descendants, but the original crossbow had long vanished and a new one created to accommodate the original bolts. She loved it though she still staked revenants as needed and had proven herself to be quite handy with so many weapons.

They all hurried forward and spread out with Dávid and Ambrus taking the perimeter toward the back and the rose garden while Éva stayed with their fathers. Once swallowed up by the unholy night, they all stopped dead in their tracks, and it had nothing to do with the dark enchantment Éva had just warned them against. In fact, the hallucinations weren't there—never happened at all—and save for the dreadful chill, all seemed calm and still around them. And very, very silent.

"There! Watch out!" Pa suddenly cried, shattering the vacuum, and Dávid turned in time to see a pale figure emerge from the ground, breaking up the mist as it clawed its way out of the soil.

It rose from under one of the unruly rose bushes littering the front grounds, tearing itself out of roots and thorns and nearly ripping the entire plant out with its painful efforts. Pa and Apa were a good distance from him and Ambrus, but they had Éva shooting without hesitation and hitting the revenant in one eye even before it could fully rise from its thorny grave. She was loading in another second while Pa lunged forward and drove a stake through the creature's chest with a furious cry.

"Dávid, hurry," Ambrus said. "They'll be fine. Have your knives out."

Dávid didn't need another urging and followed his brother to the back. The awful silence of the night was now further rent by the agonized groans and wheezes of the undead as they struggled to rise from their graves—every one of them buried under a rose bush, and Dávid's stomach coiled in nausea at the memory of those odious whispers. *We are hungry! Feed us!* Were those whispers from the cursed roses, demanding the sustenance of a master vampire's victims? Or were those from the victims themselves as they slept under thorns and plump petals, feeling their hunger grow with the waxing and waning of the moon?

"The door, Ambrus! We need to get inside!" he cried now, bolting past shivering plants and clawing hands, ghastly faces emerging from the tangle of briars, milky eyes fixed on them. "Christ, there are too many of them!"

They needed to destroy the count, Dávid knew, if they wished to weaken the undead en masse. They could only do so much on their own with just their family hunting; they'd be overwhelmed soon enough. He only hoped his fathers and sister thought along the same lines as well because if any moment required a wild burst of idiocy and recklessness, that moment would be now. It didn't help that Dávid's mind filled itself with scene after horrifying scene of what awaited him within doors. Of what might be happening to his beloved friend now.

"Lóránt, I'm coming!" he cried without thinking.

And with a powerful heave, he threw himself against the rear door once—twice—and successfully broke the old lock in his third attempt. Ambrus cheered behind him, and the two brothers were soon racing each other down a passageway blessedly lit up by spelled sconces that had been fooled into life by the count's dark magic.

Chapter 23

He'd sobbed himself to near unconsciousness, his deep and constant heaving expression of grief having sucked the air out of his lungs. And Lóránt was forced to stop himself from weeping until he'd managed to fill them again with air. It was painful. It was agony he could never put into words.

He sat bonelessly on the stairs somewhere in the middle of the tower—bloodied, disheveled, trembling, and nearly faint from the horrific moments he'd been forced to endure. Sixteen souls, he thought vaguely. He'd dispatched sixteen souls, majority of whom he recognized to be former reserves.

One of them was poor Dorika, a girl with a disfigurement—a cleft palate, Lóránt remembered. He could ill-afford to forget his peers, and while he truly didn't know some of the victims from the orphanage, he swore to himself to keep the names of those he did close to his heart. None of the dead deserved any of this—the lies that seduced them into entering a cursed household with joy in their hearts, their first death at the hands of a vampire, and now this. A second, perhaps more degrading one.

He needed to get out of there, but the fantasies kept weaving in and out of his mind, even managing to make him falter while going about his bloody business in the tower rooms he'd unlocked. He didn't know just how far he'd manage to go and whether or not exposure to the sun would affect him now that his transformation had begun. He dazedly looked down at his bloodied hands and clothes, the knife lying on the step nearby. He couldn't touch it anymore. He simply had no strength left in him, and when his numbed gaze dropped to the bloodstained key beside him, he realized he needed to dispose of it somehow before escaping.

Why is it dark? he thought, blinking, and looked up at the wall and the closest spelled sconce, which was now lit. When did that happen? It was clearly midday when he unlocked the first tower room. Surely the hours didn't pass that quickly. No—something else was going on, and with that realization, a new wave of terror swept over him, and he forced himself to stand on weakened legs. He needed to leave immediately.

He ran down the stairs, drawing strength from nothing else but the growing panic in his gut, the voiceless urging in the back of his mind pleading for him to flee the manor *now*. And once he was back on the first floor and found himself in the long gallery, the narrow windows revealed night outside though he still was left baffled as to how the time moved during his purging. *Run! He's coming!*

Lóránt bolted down the gallery. Somewhere midway through, one of the windows to his right exploded in a hail of shattered glass, and a swarm of flies flew in and overtook him. With a soundless cry, Lóránt ducked but was overrun, the swarm encasing him and pressing down while solidifying into a larger form. When he felt the awful staccato-like touches of buzzing flies against his body in one moment, it turned into an actual human body the next. Arms wrapped around him, and the momentum of a body flying into him from a different direction sent him soaring as well, and both of them tumbled and rolled several feet until they struck a wall.

"Naughty, naughty Lóránt," Count Boros hissed against his ear. "What have you done, my sweet? Playing with my servants, are you?"

Lóránt gasped at the pain of being pinned down harshly, the count's grip on his wrists crushing, and no amount of bucking and kicking bought him enough space for an effective maneuver. Like a kick in the groin, he thought in a near faint, but would that even work on a vampire as strong as his husband?

Dávid's face appeared in his terror-maddened mind again, soothing and clearing it, reminding him once more of what his beloved friend would do in such a predicament. Lóránt didn't have the advantage of size and strength, but he was agile enough, and his struggles turned frenzied, his heart hardening at the reminders of the former reserves—his peers—whom he'd just decapitated out of mercy.

Fury now took over terror, and with a snarl, Lóránt kicked and twisted, hoping his wrists would survive this assault. Count Boros laughed and pressed down for a kiss—no longer passionate and demanding, but brutal and punishing this time.

"Now come with me, darling. We have guests, you know. It won't do to be so rude."

The count stood up with unnatural strength and speed, taking Lóránt with him as though Lóránt weren't anything more than a life-sized doll. Holding him tightly against his chest but facing him still, Count Boros carried him down the rest of the way while murmuring into Lóránt's ear. Lóránt could only see what was behind the count over his shoulder.

"You were the perfect mate. Beautiful, young, and silent. Everything I ever wanted in a partner, but mistakes happen, I suppose, as I didn't expect you to be such a feisty little thing. I'll have to start over somewhere—again—perhaps France since I love that place so much. A French beauty would be good, and if he isn't born mute, I'll have to cut his tongue out myself. Perhaps do something with his brain as well if I expect full submission from him. Yes, that's giving me ideas, my sweet silence. I understand doctors in lunatic asylums do things to patients' brains to render them quiet and obedient, which I suspect is more effective than casting spells on them. I'll have to look into that, but first—I'm afraid our marriage is over, Lóránt. And what a dreadful shame it is."

Lóránt struggled in his husband's arms, barely keeping up with the count's monologue as he was carried out onto the grand staircase. His right hand managed to inch down, his jacket pocket within reach, and he stuck his hand in just when the count abruptly stopped on the main landing.

"Get back if you want him alive," Count Boros cried, his voice sounding almost scattered and diffused—as though he spoke with more than one voice. His hold tightened, squeezing Lóránt painfully until Lóránt's vision wove in and out of focus. He couldn't move in spite of his efforts, the count being impossibly strong and vicious, and his breaths were starting to hitch from a mix of punishing pressure and panic.

"Lóránt! Don't you fucking dare, you fucking monster! Let him go!"

Dávid? Lóránt blinked weakly at the wall behind the count. Dávid was here?

"Ah, how delightful—you brought guests! Welcome, friends! Here to see the happy couple, are you? I'm afraid you're all too late, though, because the honeymoon's quite over."

"Oh, we know that. Let him go, and we'll make your death nice and easy," another voice—male—said.

"Why the hell is he covered in blood?" Dávid all but howled in fury. "What did you do to him?"

"Nothing yet. I assure you, I found him like this. Covered in my servants' gore. See, this is grounds for separation, don't you agree? I leave my servants to his care, and what does he do? Slaughter them in cold blood. So vicious. So naughty. Rather delicious, though."

Lóránt, limp and wracked with pain, felt the hold around him loosen, the iron bands crushing his bones ease and shift so that he was moved across Count Boros's front. He immediately fumbled for the rosary in his pocket, found it, and gripped it tightly. Something told him the count, in his arrogance, was about to do something before Dávid and whoever else was there—a final and fitting punishment for Lóránt, something designed to humiliate him before Dávid. Then escape with an ease born of centuries' worth of a cursed existence. Lóránt would, if he could, have laughed at himself for entertaining such outlandish ideas, but fireside tales meant to frighten children reigned supreme now while reason and science were forced back into the shadows.

Lóránt's feet couldn't feel the floor. He was being held up literally in space, given his much smaller stature, and once the count was done with him, he'd be dropped to his death.

"Don't fret, everyone," Count Boros said, his voice diffusing further, and this time the hum of invisible flies added a grotesque layer to his sound. "Just one last kiss goodbye, and I'll be parting ways with my darling."

He moved swiftly then, plunging his fangs into the wounds in Lóránt's throat, and there it was again—the icy burn, the unbelievable pain, and the inevitable weakening of Lóránt's body as the count drank greedily. *Do it. Do it for yourself.* Yes, rest sounded quite good. He needed rest desperately, and now was his chance to have it at last. No more pain, no more loneliness—no more grief that crippled him from within.

He could barely make sense of the noise exploding around him—voices raised in horror and rage, with Dávid shrieking his fury so loudly his voice shattered. Several voices joined his as well, a mix of male and female voices, perhaps two or three calling upon St. Michael. There were shouted commands like "Stay with him! We'll take care of the others!" Another sounded like "He'll turn into another swarm—be ready for it!" A woman said in a calm and steady voice, "I have him."

Lóránt felt his grip on the rosary loosening as his consciousness slipped, and right at that moment, the count tore away from his throat with a wet howl. The sound of something slicing through space had rent the air a second before, the next moment seemed to happen as though time slowed to a painful crawl, and Lóránt was able to witness everything despite his fading awareness.

A small arrow-like thing had been shot from somewhere, the aim sure and true, and it pierced the side of the count's neck. It made him pull out of Lóránt's throat, his bloodied mouth wide open, and it was then when Lóránt struck with his final strength.

He shoved the rosary into the gaping mouth, forcing it in with every ounce of energy he could muster, and almost immediately he saw the effects of a blessed artifact of faith on a creature of unholy origins as smoke rose from the count's face. Was the rosary carved out of an ash tree? Lóránt had heard about the wood's use as the primary material for vampire stakes, and he'd have wondered irrationally at that in spite of the surreal events he was now caught up in had he not felt himself lifted and then dropped.

Count Boros had once again turned into a swarm of flies, and the loss of his physical human body left Lóránt falling in space. He was going to break his neck once and for all, he thought fuzzily. All the while the noise around him intensified with more shouts, more prayers, more wild movement. The world spun, the pain up and down his body made him wish for a quick death, and his fading vision barely noted flashes of light and then a sudden burst of fire.

But why wasn't he falling now? Why was he lying on something softer than a stone floor?

"Lóránt, Lóránt, I'm here. I finally got you. Everything will be all right, I swear. I'm sorry it took me so long to find you. I'm so sorry." Dávid was heaven on earth, Lóránt decided just as darkness took him. Dávid was an angel, and maybe he was there to take Lóránt back to where it was peace and light and endless joy.

Chapter 24

Dear God, Lóránt looked like hell, Dávid thought as he held his friend firmly against himself. It had been touch and go, dashing up the rest of the stairs just when the count vanished into a disgusting swarm of flies almost immediately after Éva's bolt pierced his neck.

Dávid had inched up the stairs, step by step, his gaze fixed on the doll-like figure of Lóránt as the boy hung weakly from his husband's arms, held close in a mockery of an embrace, his throat being savaged by a beast deserving to be put down in the worst possible way. If Boros were to drop Lóránt, it would send the boy's body bouncing in the most sickening way down the stairs and to the bottom. Lóránt, barely alive, wouldn't survive the first impact, Dávid was sure.

But there was no need to dwell on what never happened. It was nothing short of a miracle he was now holding his friend—no, damn him, *his Lóránt!*—in his arms at last, alive but significantly altered. So beautiful, his Lóránt—he was so beautiful. Dávid's heart, already cracked in so many places, struggled to fix itself as he chased after more pleasant thoughts of what he and Lóránt could do together once the latter was healed and whole and back to his old self. But was there any going back to the old self after this, though? Dávid took a shuddering breath and gently brushed a kiss on Lóránt's cold forehead.

Perhaps it was good for the heart to delude oneself with happy, improbable dreams.

He blinked back the gathering tears as he stayed on the stairs, watching his family and their unlooked-for reinforcements destroy what remained of Count Boros's "children". Creations, more like.

He watched Ambrus, roaring like a god of war, as he took down one more vampire that had skittered out of reach, crawling like a ghastly lizard on the black wall while hissing viciously. Ambrus had thrown a dagger and struck the creature's back, sending it toppling backward and landing in a heap near his feet. Ambrus had stepped on the squirming revenant, repositioned the bloodied stake he'd pulled out of another corpse, and struck without needing a mallet. He was *that* strong, which left Dávid marveling, and with the stake came the near-simultaneous swing of the blade. It was over in mere seconds—a hunter at his best.

Éva bounced around between the interior and outside, still lending incredible support with her unearthly precision with her hand crossbow. And apparently she didn't need to dive in and lend a hand at staking revenants, thanks largely for the unexpected arrival of the Stasiuk family—mother, father, twin brothers, and Irén—supreme masters of the arcane arts, casting spells left and right with an accuracy that rivaled Éva's.

From what Dávid had gathered through scattered bits of information during the fights, it was Count Boros's attempts at creating a new hive elsewhere that had been the hunt the family had gotten embroiled in prior to this.

And when Boros suddenly fled, dissolving into flies and heading straight for this place, the family gave chase. Destroying a master vampire would make hunting for the rest of the hive a great deal easier for everyone, and heaven only knew how many he'd been able to form, which had led to the resurgence of vampire infestations all over the Kingdom of Hungary as well as Poland.

"Fuck me, those things coming out from under the roses were dressed as though they're about to go to a grand ball," Ambrus said, dragging a hand across his sweaty and soiled brow. He panted as he rested against the balustrade for a bit, his gaze moving all over. "How's Lóránt?"

"I need Pa," Dávid replied. His arms felt numb from the weight and from holding them still for so long now, but he refused to surrender his burden. "Lóránt needs some preliminary spell to ease the bite's effects—and other things. I don't know what he endured living here—even for less than a month." He tried for a more detached observation, but instead, he burst into tears. "It's my fault. I should have looked for him sooner. I always had the upperhand—like money and resources and all that. I even promised him in my letters," he stammered, his words coming out in fits and starts while Ambrus listened in grave silence, sympathy in his eyes. "He looks so bad, Ambrus. I don't want him to die."

"And we won't let him," Pa's voice cut through the cloud of grief that now had Dávid in its dreadful grip. "Dávid? It's me. May I take a quick look? Ah—all right. It looks like all the blood on him isn't his. That's good. His throat worries me, though. I don't know if he's been made to drink the count's blood, but—all right."

Pa placed a soiled hand on Lóránt's forehead and the other on his throat. He then murmured a prayer—perhaps a prayer-spell—in Latin, his face a picture of intense concentration. After a minute or so, he took his hands away and smiled at Dávid. "He'll be all right, Dávid. We can't move him for now, but Julek and Zofia are cleansing the ground floor to make the rooms livable temporarily. We can at least settle in for the night and rest."

"What about Lóránt?" Dávid asked, sighing heavily in relief. He raised Lóránt a little to bury his lips in his friend's hair. "Are we sending for a doctor?"

"We have Piotr and Roman's talents, so don't worry. The healing Lóránt requires goes beyond a doctor's skills—we have to accept that." Pa paused and smiled affectionately, this time stroking Dávid's tear-stained cheek with his fingers—fingers that had destroyed undead creatures not too long ago without a shred of mercy or hesitation. "This is your reality now, I'm afraid. Yours and Lóránt's."

Dávid nodded. "It's all right. I suppose—I suppose if I ought to learn anything from all this, it's that I desperately need more training. I was practically useless tonight—couldn't help it when I saw him."

Pa laughed gently now. "And you'll get it. With any luck, with your Lóránt by your side as I suspect—and I do hope I'm wrong—his unfinished transformation might have linked him psychically to the undead. If you're a hunter, he'll be your mental connection to the otherworld, something like a seer and yet not. He'll know instinctively revenants' movements within a certain distance, so at least there's a limit to this—unexpected and, I suppose, unwanted—ability."

"I don't want him dragged into this again, Pa. I don't."

"I know you don't. No one does. But I thought to warn you, anyway, because everything I've read about these partial transformations point in that direction. It might yet be undone, though, and that's where our Polish friends come in with their expertise."

Pa smiled again, reassuring Dávid with his unwavering love and feeding the hope in Dávid's heart. No, indeed—if Dávid could help it, Lóránt wasn't going to be involved whatsoever in future hunts, seer or no seer—unless he wished it.

Mr. and Mrs. Stasiuk then appeared, looking quite pleased in spite of their atrocious states, but such was the way of those who'd taken the oath to defend mortals against an unholy army. Their work would never be done, and Dávid was nothing if not proud as hell to be caught up in the never ending cycle as new generations were introduced and trained. And, apparently, some were even outperforming their sires, which only added to the relief and reassurance among the older hunters: yes, their work was certainly in good hands, and there was much hope for the future once the time came for them to lay their weapons down.

The revenants infesting the grounds had been thoroughly dispatched, leaving carnage everywhere with several rose bushes suffering catastrophically. The sunrise would reduce all those bodies to ash; the Stasiuk twins, Piotr and Roman, ensured it with the prayer-spells they'd cast after the coast was declared clear. Apa, Pa, Irén, and Éva all fetched the horses and brought them to the wood for safety, taking care to keep the animals from the grounds where all the destruction took place. Irén, who was now becoming an expert spell-caster herself, blessed the wood further because she turned out to be the softest heart when it came to animals.

If only his reunion with his childhood friend happened under better, happier circumstances, Dávid thought as they gathered for an impromptu supper in the banquet room. Ordinary mortal fare had been discovered in the kitchen, which then led to soup—because no one could roast fowl if their lives depended on it—with a generous side of bread and cheese. Dávid refused to join them, however, opting instead to eat his food at Lóránt's bedside, which was a sofa that had been turned into a comfortable nest with blankets and pillows.

"I'm sorry for not joining you tonight," he'd said as he stood awkwardly in the doorway to the banquet room. "But—I don't want to miss the moment when he opens his eyes, you know?"

It was Irén who'd insisted upon bringing his supper tray, and she smiled at him when she withdrew. "He'll be all right, Dávid," she said. "And you know we'll be here for him."

Pa came by twice more before retiring for the night to cast another healing spell on the patient. More prayers to St. Michael were said, more supplications for Lóránt's healing. Before long the château was silent—and in a more mundane way, at that.

No, actually, Dávid reminded himself with a yawn. Not château. Irén had corrected him as only an intellectual would by referring to the structure as a manor house and something about troubadours and France and other such fussy nonsense. Well, château or manor house, it certainly felt like a normal domicile now, quite free of dark influences that had brought about its existence and kept it standing.

Dávid himself couldn't sleep and still sat beside Lóránt, and this time he took a book out from the library and proceeded to read to his slumbering friend in as quiet and soothing a voice as he could. If Lóránt needed happier dreams, Dávid was there to feed his mind with the most colorful, most humorous, and most romantic stories he could find—surprisingly enough, original fairy tales from the Kingdom of Hungary, penned by an author who apparently had his head in the clouds all day, every day, and Dávid loved every story.

"The fellow who wrote these stories reminds me of you," he whispered with a watery smile. "Look at all these daydreams!"

Since none of the clocks in the manor house worked, Dávid didn't know what time it was exactly when Lóránt came back to him. But he was in the middle of reading a story somewhere halfway through the book when he felt a gentle touch on a cheek. Startled, he glanced up to find Lóránt watching him with those large but tired eyes of his, his mouth curved in a shy smile. It took Dávid a wretchedly long time just gaping stupidly at Lóránt before shaking himself and taking hold of the hand that had drawn his attention away.

But Lóránt apparent was also struggling to communicate something, and when Dávid reluctantly released his hand, he languidly signed "I liked kissing you" while blushing. Dávid, overwhelmed, could only answer by taking one thin hand again and pressing a fervent kiss on the pale skin. Once, twice, three times—and more.

Chapter 25

The path to healing from a vampire's bite and the dark spell that had been cast in an effort to keep him docile proved to be worse than the ordeal of being cursed by attracting a vampire's attention to begin with.

Vicious remnants of the enchantment Count Boros had nearly crippled him with dogged Lóránt's hours. So many ghastly images of things he didn't even have words for came and went, emerging from the darkest shadows of the room and at times drawing terrified voiceless shrieks from him. He'd woken up a few times flailing and attempting to crawl off the bed while still caught in the grip of a black dream, only to be stopped and held fast by Dávid, who never failed to rouse Lóránt completely from the depths with his voice and his gentle calls.

"Come back to me. I'm here, sweetheart. It was only a dream. Nothing's going to hurt you anymore, I swear. Ah, there he is," Dávid would murmur while holding him close and rocking him lightly, his lips pressed against Lóránt's damp forehead.

Years of a monster's mental drugging required a month of intensive healing and care, apparently, which included an equally intense and thorough treatment of a vampire's bite. Lóránt was fortunate he never reached that step of being seduced into drinking the count's blood since that would have completed his turning—and Dávid would have been gone forever. Even worse, Dávid would have been forced to hunt him down and destroy him. But the moment had been close—too close, in fact.

"You can't dwell on something that never happened, young man," Mr. Gárdonyi—the gentleman with the scar—said once Lóránt's recovery was nearly complete.

He sat on the bed beside Lóránt, who'd propped himself up with large and very comfortable pillows so he could sit properly in deference to Dávid's apa. But to his surprise, Mr. Gárdonyi merely kicked his shoes off and settled himself beside Lóránt, stretching his long legs out and crossing them at the ankles. A picture of gentlemanly indolence.

"And it never will. The only worry we all have is whether or not you're left with some psychic connection to the world of the undead since you've been bitten."

Lóránt thoughtfully touched his neck, which was whole again and didn't even have scars, thanks to the combined efforts of more than one spell-casting hunter—including an entire family from Warsaw. He sighed and gestured. "No. I had nightmares of the count, but they were all about the manor house and the servants. He was chasing me all over the place, and I couldn't get away."

"Good. He's gone now, and that should help further your healing. However, should you feel anything—unusual—something like a quiet warning in your head that you don't understand. A portent of some distant danger or something like that. Don't hesitate to speak up, all right? We've chased down and destroyed Boros, but other threats are still out there, and if the literature we've read about aborted transformations are true, this ability to sense the presence of a revenant might have been forced on you, I'm afraid," Mr. Gárdonyi said, and he took one of Lóránt's hands in his for a reassuring squeeze. "But you're not alone in this, Lóránt. Remember that."

The bedroom door swung open just at that moment, and a beaming Dávid stood there, carrying a tray of tea and sweetbread. "Snack time!" he cheerfully announced.

"And that's my cue to abandon you." Mr. Gárdonyi got up and grinned at Lóránt. "You're doing very well, young man. Keep it up."

How could Lóránt not be inspired to make the effort? With Dávid striding toward the bed, his chest puffed like a proud peacock because, apparently, he made the sweetbread himself for Lóránt—how could he not heal so quickly? This fiery, kind-hearted giant of a gentleman had become the center of Lóránt's world going several years back. Lóránt couldn't imagine a world without Dávid Gárdonyi, and he was certain—though Dávid would likely tease him for being a hopeless romantic—the day when Dávid left Lóránt's world forever would be the day when Lóránt himself would cease to exist.

His appetite enjoyed a resurgence, even an improvement, but he'd point to the remarkable skill of the cook for rousing his body's need for sustenance and even making it a very enjoyable experience. What he'd been fed at the manor house was nothing compared to the food served here.

It also helped that Dávid was giving him his full attention every time the meal tray was brought to him, ensuring Lóránt ate till he was full regardless of whether or not he finished his meal. There was an affection there—an expression of love—that went beyond mere friendship, he suspected, judging from the shifting light in Dávid's eyes, whose gaze seemed almost reverential. Worshipful. And being the object of such adoring scrutiny never failed to make Lóránt blush and awaken his heart to sensations he'd at first thought to be alien but were really the result of a natural progression.

His face burned even more as he ate his sweetbread, his thoughts fully on the gentleman—yes, Dávid was a gentleman now, not the scruffy orphan who'd engage in fistfights on Lóránt's behalf—who was taking very good care of him day after day. Bringing him food, ensuring a servant helped Lóránt wash himself, reading to him, and bringing news from the outside world to him.

And heaven help him, Lóránt had fallen madly in love with his friend. Perhaps he'd always been in his own childish, insignificant way before, but he'd never understood the nature of his affection for his one and only friend—even dismissed it more than once as nothing more than a pitiful dependence born of loneliness. Now, however, he knew it was a great deal more complicated than that, and he was perfectly fine with it, much to his surprise.

"What are you smiling about now? Is the sweetbread that good? I figured it would be," Dávid said, and Lóránt laughed. Even those wheezing sounds he made—the subject of so much childhood shame—no longer bothered him.

"No, it's something better," he signed, blushing furiously now. "I like being with you."

"Good because I like being with you, too."

Well, that was a step in the right direction, and Lóránt knew better than to rush things. He redirected the conversation to more serious things now that he was nearly completely healed and more than ready to leave the sickroom and move around some more. Hobbling about in such a confined space helped, but he desperately wished for the open air and a thorough exploration of the grounds. This was Dávid's home, after all, and Lóránt was a special guest until he found work and established himself independently. And in order to get to that point, he needed to get his strength back and eventually explore his options with the help of his hosts.

"The château..." Dávid paused and rolled his eyes. "Fucking manor house, I mean—its grounds are now purified."

According to him, the manor house, in spite of its gorgeous architecture and marvelous construction, was still a cursed space and was therefore razed to the ground, the corpses of the servants still inside. That was the only way to end that chapter of Count Boros's existence as well as to fully liberate those unfortunate souls Lóránt was forced to destroy a second time. The bodies of the revenants the hunters had decimated the fateful day of Lóránt's near death were left to the sun's natural purifying power, and in another fortnight, the grounds were as empty and silent as though no one had ever lived there, the charred and crumbling walls of the manor house fated to be overrun by Nature over time until they all but vanished from knowledge.

It had been easier than expected, hunting Count Boros down and cornering him for destruction. He was injured by Éva's blessed bolt and Sr. Beáta's rosary, the latter being left behind by the count after he transformed into a swarm of flies, and Lóránt received it slightly charred and stained with his own blood. He refused to take it back, of course, and it was put away somewhere in the reliquary room. As suspected, the rosary was made from an ash tree, and Dávid thought Lóránt forcing the rosary into the vampire's wide open mouth as Boros howled in pain from Éva's bolt was a "genius move". He only got a disgusted shudder and a scowl from Lóránt.

"I was allowed the killing blow," Dávid said in a quiet and somber manner. He held Lóránt's hand in his, the tray of food already taken away and set aside. "Éva shot him a couple of times again to slow him down some more, but everyone stepped back, and I knew they wanted me to finish him off. They didn't even have to say a word to me."

"It must have been a nightmare," Lóránt signed with some difficulty since Dávid seemed unwilling to release his hand. "I'm sorry you had to endure it."

"I'm not. He deserved it a thousand times over, and I'd do it again and again and again. I just kept thinking of all those orphans who were fed to him when they thought they finally had a real chance at a better life. They'll never grow old like us. They'll never know how it's like to be parents or grandparents or just older single people with happier lives ahead of them and behind them." Dávid swallowed, and the gaze he fixed on Lóránt was almost despairing. "But I thought of you most of all. Everything you went through—all the pain you had to suffer even before you got his attention when you were only a child. All the nightmares you had to endure because he wanted you not just silent, but impossibly subservient. You never spent a single day without being manipulated in some way or another, Lóránt. And I wanted to destroy him over and over again for taking so much away from you."

Lóránt smiled through his tears. "I thought of you, too. All those days in the manor house—I thought of you. You were the only thing that kept me from succumbing to madness. You helped me find the strength to do what I had to do to those poor servants. And the rosary—actually, no. That genius move was entirely mine. I'm afraid you can't take credit for inspiring me at that moment."

Dávid guffawed, shaking his head. "No, no, you're right. You deserve full credit for that. Ambrus already wrote that down in his journal because we're all determined to ensure it's never forgotten."

"Quite fitting we had each other to draw our courage from, isn't it?"

Dávid hesitated, his gaze dropping to Lóránt's hands as they rested on his lap. "One can't help it, I suppose, when one's in love," he said. He took a deep breath and looked up, terror in his eyes with his heart laid open and all its secrets exposed for Lóránt to do what he would with them. "I'm in love with you, Lóránt. I really am."

The tears wouldn't stop, but it was easier to smile through them. "Oh, are you now? See, I don't know if I believe it. I think I'll need some convincing. A proper kiss would do it," he signed.

And Dávid being Dávid, he obliged wholeheartedly and pulled Lóránt, unresisting, into his arms. So there, Lóránt thought as he melted into the kiss, there at last was the promised adventure down the moon-blessed river and its gentle currents.

Chapter 26

"That would have to be the quickest and most effective hunt we've ever had," Éva said as she dismounted from her horse, giving the cherished animal a loving stroke before surrendering it to one of the servants. She glanced at Dávid, who felt he'd just aged fifty more years, judging from the way his bones screamed when he tried to move. He'd never get used to riding horses at great distances. Never. "Thank Lóránt for us, of course."

"I will, but I shouldn't. He's grown too big-headed for his own good."

Éva and Ambrus laughed as they strode into the great house, the smell of supper filling Dávid's nostrils and heart with the promise of home and family. And Lóránt, of course. Ambrus went off to search for their fathers to give them a full account of that evening's hunt—a brief, brutal, but shockingly easy one, thanks in large part to Lóránt's acquired ability to sense revenants' presence within a greater distance than expected.

The ability didn't manifest itself right away; indeed, it seemed to have lain dormant for a while as though waiting for Lóránt to be fully cleansed of Count Boros's nightmare influence. The fantasies were gone as well as the bite, and the nightmares gradually stopped—though not soon enough as far as Dávid was concerned.

Another fortnight or so passed following Pa's declaration of Lóránt's complete recovery before the initial stirrings of unease troubled Lóránt's waking hours. They were very subtle nudges in the back of his mind, and the feeling of overriding horror was surprisingly light but insistent. Vague and yet strong enough to impress a certain muted urgency in Lóránt's mind, and Lóránt would be seeking one of the family out to tell them.

"They're here," he'd sign. "They've come."

The crows would then be engaged for a reconnaissance, and another hunt would be planned.

Dávid made good his promise not to involve Lóránt in the hunts even with his ability. He was stuck at home—willingly, at least, since his encounters with the undead had been far worse than any of Dávid's family could claim for theirs.

"I'm not a hunter. I'll never be one, and I don't want to be one, Dávid. I can't do it again—use a knife in that way, and—I just can't," he confessed tearfully, and Dávid had to hold him close and reassure him over and over again until Lóránt finally realized he wasn't being forced into the world of hunters. Not physically, no, but at least as the unexpected conduit between two worlds, Lóránt gladly volunteered himself as a psychic tracker of sorts.

Apa and Pa, both of whom had slowly stepped away from hunts now that Dávid had improved his skills and learned to control his reckless turns in these fights, took Lóránt under their wing and taught him how best to master this unexpected but effective ability. They all read more literature together, and Lóránt's insatiable appetite for knowledge also led him to hours lost in the reliquary room, devouring book after book as long as he knew the language.

Over time, Lóránt learned to embrace his ability. This lingering and permanent mental scar from his life with the count despite its merciful brevity—it was a form of mind rape he'd redefined and reshaped to his advantage, using it to its fullest potential as a means of protection through prevention.

"I might as well make the bastard useful, yes?" Lóránt signed, his wedding ring glinting in the soft light and stirring Dávid's happiness all over again. He loved this remarkable creature—his strength and courage, his ability to adapt with such astonishing speed. The goodness in his heart that was never dimmed or shattered even as life battered mercilessly at it. Dávid could only hope to prove himself worthy of Lóránt's love.

Dávid took Ambrus's bag and brought it back to the reliquary room to put away along with his own tools. Éva went off to wash up for supper, and Dávid hobbled toward the rear of the great house and up to what he now fondly called his turret home.

It was his and Lóránt's assigned home now that they were married—one of the two round towers of the house, and they were given the key to the entire structure, which meant the three floors and their generously lit interiors were his and Lóránt's to do what they would with them. This arrangement allowed them their privacy as a pair, of course, and they had a choice as to whether or not to eat their meals alone or to join the family in the dining-room. So far they enjoyed breakfast together and lunch and supper with the others.

"I heard you grunting up those stairs," Lóránt observed with a badly suppressed smile and fluttery gestures.

He sat flanked by books at the small table on the first floor of the tower, which was their main living space. The table also worked multiple duties for meals and work, and Lóránt often spent his time balancing Dávid's ledgers from his business there, Piri curled on his lap. That was exactly what he was doing that evening, looking just as beautiful as ever in spite of two years of married life putting up with Dávid's excessive doting and—rather wild lovemaking that left poor Lóránt happily wrecked and barely able to walk for half a day after.

"I'll never get used to horseback riding," Dávid replied with an exaggerated groan, and he bent down to kiss his husband. "It's good to be home. Éva thanks you again for your help. Tonight's hunt was over before we even knew it."

Lóránt grinned and pulled Dávid back down for a few more kisses. "Good," he signed after releasing him. "The sooner you come home safe and in one piece, the sooner I'm able to berate you for your awful math because these accounts are atrocious."

"Ah, well—then I'll have to make things up to you. I'm awfully good at apologizing, you know."

Dávid's grin broadened as he bent down again, locked his arms around Lóránt's waist, and lifted him off the chair, Lóránt laughing his delight as he wrapped his legs around Dávid's middle. Dávid would never get tired of this, grateful as ever for the size difference between them even though Lóránt was technically a tall enough fellow, but he seemed to be fashioned from air and was more fairy-like than mortal. He barely made Dávid huff as he was carried to a spacious part of the room and gently laid on the floor.

"We're doing it here and not upstairs?" Lóránt's clumsy gestures suggested a stammered question.

"Of course. I owe you an apology for all those mathematical corrections you had to do to save my business, and it's an apology that's rather time sensitive and shouldn't be put off another minute." Dávid sat up and tore away at his clothes and then at Lóránt's, barely noting all the buttons flying in every direction as heat and lust threatened to turn him feral while Lóránt laughed himself silly.

"The oil!" Lóránt stared at Dávid's erection. "I'm not taking that monster in without it!"

They were, of course, late for supper, but at least the family waited. The little smirks and genteel coughs as they entered the dining-room—slightly disheveled and hastily dressed so that some of the buttons were in the wrong buttonholes—suggested a tolerance that could only be allowed for young married couples. Lóránt certainly looked well-fucked and utterly delectable, and Dávid preened as he pulled the chair out for his still-dazed husband, whose complaints over Dávid's wretched math skills seemed to have been forgotten for now.

Apa had been reading a letter before they joined the family, and it lay opened beside his plate.

"What news, Apa?" Éva prodded once they were all seated.

Dávid wasn't sure, but he suspected everyone purposefully ignored the way Lóránt gingerly lowered himself to his chair before glaring at Dávid once he was seated. Dávid could only drop a kiss into his slightly tousled hair in apology before taking his place beside his husband.

"A few items from Zofia Stasiuk," Apa said. He picked up the letter again while everyone served themselves. "The twins are away with Julek on a support hunt in Bucharest. There've been rumors of a growing infestation over there, reports of revenants emerging from the plague of the earlier years of this century. Or at least the belief is that the plague from years past is now being blamed for the possible appearance of revenants in the city. Julek and his sons will be gathering information and offering their knowledge—as they always do.

"Irén, by the bye, is insistent upon working with Lóránt since he's quite the scholar. She'll be writing you, of course, to discuss matters in greater detail and see if you'd be interested. You've proven to be invaluable help to her family, and she wishes to secure the future." Apa glanced up at Lóránt now and smiled wryly. "I'm afraid you're being slowly dragged into the family business, son, regardless. But it's up to you to decide."

Lóránt looked at Dávid, lower lip caught between his teeth as he considered, uncertainty in his eyes. At Dávid's fond smile, he breathed out a sigh of relief.

"I'd be happy to," he signed with a touch of energy and eagerness in his gestures now, delighted and saucer-eyed. "If that means I'm able to help in some way, information is just as good as strength and skill with weaponry, right? Does that mean I get to be an archivist, too?"

Dávid sighed. There was no holding him back, apparently, now that he'd found his confidence, and he'd survived a grotesque nightmare of a trial by fire. He never once expected his little friend—no longer little but still a friend and also a great deal more—to prove himself everyone's equal when staring into the blackest depths of Hell, but there he was, and Dávid couldn't be any prouder.

So much choice had been denied Lóránt since their childhood, and Dávid wanted nothing more than to give him all the autonomy he needed from this point on. Besides, it would also allow Dávid to watch from a careful distance, be his husband's protector whenever the situation required it, and quietly let his love and gratitude grow with every passing day.

"St. Jerome's is on the road to recovery under a new director, but previous staff have been replaced save for the nurse. The orphanage suffered a good deal of legal nightmares from the previous administration's tenure—nearly got shut down, in fact. There are no reserves," Apa continued, a grimace of revulsion darkening his features at the mention of reserves, "and those children with physical challenges are looked after by a new set of tutors and a nurse specifically trained in their needs. Good to know!"

And so on and so forth. Dávid settled in comfortably and ate his supper in utmost contentment, awash in the comfort that could only come from being in the company of the people who mattered to him the most.

The moonlit hunts would continue, of course, because human nature's weakness in the face of riches and opportunities, consequences be damned, was as eternal as the sun and the moon. But they'd face it without fear—they'd done so before, and they'd do so again, with Dávid's fixed point at his side: Lóránt Gárdonyi, who was just as eternal as the sun and the moon in Dávid's shameless, overly biased opinion.

Don't miss out!

Visit the website below and you can sign up to receive emails whenever Hayden Thorne publishes a new book. There's no charge and no obligation.

https://books2read.com/r/B-A-LFQC-NHRUD

About the Author

I've lived most of my life in the San Francisco Bay Area though I wasn't born there (or, indeed, the USA). I'm married with no kids and three cats.

I started off as a writer of gay young adult fiction, specializing in contemporary fantasy, historical fantasy, and historical genres. My books ranged from a superhero fantasy series to reworked and original folktales to Victorian ghost fiction.

I've since expanded to gay New Adult fiction, which reflects similar themes as my YA books and varies considerably in terms of romantic and sexual content.

While I've published with a small press in the past, I now self-publish my books. Please visit my site for exclusive sales and publishing updates.

Read more at https://www.haydenthorne.com.

www.ingramcontent.com/pod-product-compliance
Lightning Source LLC
Chambersburg PA
CBHW021215130726
47988CB00002B/671